necessary
Lies

necessary Lies

11/13/16

Dear Kerry —
For everything. And for everything
again —
words, deeds,
feeling, travel,
meals, and
and and ....
XOXO
Kerry

WINNER OF THE G.S. SHARAT CHANDRA
PRIZE FOR SHORT FICTION

SELECTED BY HILARY MASTERS

KERRY NEVILLE BAKKEN

BkMk Press
University of Missouri-Kansas City

BkMk Press
University of Missouri-Kansas City
5101 Rockhill Road
Kansas City, MO 64110-2499
(816) 235-2558 (voice); (816)235-2611 (fax)
bkmk press@umkc.edu   www.umkc.edu/bkmk

Cover design: Aleksandra Beshkova
Author photo: Bill Owens
Book interior design: Susan L. Schurman
Managing Editor: Ben Furnish
Printing: Walsworth Publishing Company, Marceline, Missouri

BkMk Press wishes to thank: Bill Beeson, Teresa Collins,
Christopher Glenn, Andrés Rodríguez, Kate Melles,
Heather Clark, Matthew Foust, J.J. Cantrell, Rachel K. Hiles

The G.S. Sharat Chandra Prize for Short Fiction wishes to thank:
J.J. Cantrell, Elizabeth Smith, Leslie Koffler, Linda Rodriguez

Library of Congress Catlaoging-in-Publication Data

Bakken, Kerry Neville
    Necessary lies / Kerry Neville Bakken.
        p. cm.
    Summary: " A collection of seven short-stories that
examines how suicide, divorce, infidelity, infertility, and lies affect
several middle-class, Northeastern American families in the late
20th century"—Provided by publisher.
    ISBN 1-886157-56-1 (pbk.: alk. paper) 1. Domestic
fiction, American. 2. Middle class families—Fiction. 3. New
England—Social life and customs—20th century—Fiction.
I. Title.
        PS3602.A592N43 2006
        813'.6—dc22   2006014739

ACKNOWLEDGMENTS

The stories in this collection were originally published as follows:

"The Effects of Light"—*Glimmer Train*

"Necessary Lies"—*Story Quarterly*

"Eggs"—*Fourth River*

"Remains"—*The Cimarron Review*

"The Body/Love Problem," "Vigil," and "Renter's Guide to the Hamptons"—*Hampton Shorts Journal*

I am grateful for the extraordinary guidance and friendship of Frederick Busch and Daniel Stern, and for the invaluable help and encouragement of Anne Borchardt, my agent. I am honored that Hilary Masters selected this manuscript for the G.S. Sharat Chandra Prize and lucky my manuscript landed into the wonderfully wise hands of Ben Furnish, J.J. Cantrell, Susan Schurman, Teresa Collins, Bill Beeson, and Robert Stewart at BkMk Press. I am thankful for the friendship of Erin Jensen, Amy Taylor, Corey Marks, Gloria Stern, and Karen and Oscar Seibel, my magnificent parents-in-law. And, of course, thanks to my family for their support and patience over all these years: my sister, Erin Colello, who listened to my stories even when they were about strange elves who lived in ears; my brother, Colin Neville, who has become one of my most intuitive and helpful readers; and my parents, Susan and Martin Neville, who always let me stay up past bedtime reading into the night. And always, my gratitude to Christopher Bakken, who every day makes this possible, and to my children Sophia and Alexander, who make this worthwhile.

For Christopher, and in memory of Frederick Busch.

The voice in *Necessary Lies* and its speaker's clarity of vision are implicit in almost every page. I hear this voice. The wit, in all the senses of that word, that impels the different narratives creates an immediate intimacy with the reader. This is a wise, contemporary intellect that assesses the hard facts of our time as well as the trivia sometimes taken for hard facts.

—Hilary Masters
   Final Judge
   G. S. Sharat Chandra Prize for Short Fiction

necessary Lies

THE EFFECTS OF LIGHT

*All material in nature, the mountains and the streams and the air and
we, are made of light which has been spent, and this crumpled mass called
material casts a shadow, and this shadow belongs to light.—Louis Kahn*

The air conditioning quit hours ago, so like
dogs we stick our faces out the cracked
windows of the bus, panting into the wind.
Too many times we have had to stop at dingy gas stations
for little cups of coffee, cigarettes, and greasy spanakopita.
Or for pile-ups of goats glaring in the middle of the road,
jangling their bells in admonition. Or once for the driver to
take a slow deliberate piss into a field of yellow wildflowers.
I admired his swagger as he reboarded the bus, shrugging,
still working on his belt buckle.

Sarah emphatically did not. "Disgusting," she said. All
afternoon she has been staring into hills shaggy with cypress
trees, then at the cliffs, the edges of Mount Zas, and the sea.
Her long blond hair is clipped up in an unbrushed tangle,
her neck and cheeks flushed, sunburned. She looks lovely
and alone, as if she's been traveling forever, like one of those

colonial heroines lollygagging about India or Morocco, churning up the copper dust with her heavy skirts. Though Sarah is with me here, it is right that she appears as if she is not: we are divorcing. I no longer have a claim.

The rest of the passengers, the Greeks, have kept their curtains drawn against the sharp sunlight. Not Sarah. Of all people, Sarah should know better. She, the expert on the effects of light, her life's work, wandering from one small town museum or historic mansion to another, calculating the sun's cumulative damage on textiles and watercolors, bleached sideboards and yellowed draperies. Now, though, her fingers curl and flex in the light as if she is trying to palm its energy, store it up.

I take up two seats: one for my ass, one for my leg. The widows on the bus *tsk tsk* my indolence, my American gall, then see the gangly crutches propped against the window, perhaps even notice my face blanch and tighten as the bus jounces over ruts. Do they hear the sharp intake of breath and turn, as Sarah does at a particularly bad spot in the road and my spine and knee and ankle summon up the fall once again down all those flights of stairs, the breaks, the unnatural angle of repose? I grit my teeth. All I can do is ride it out.

Sarah says, "All of that out there is broom."

"Broom?" I ask.

"Those yellow flowers. They're supposed to smell like honey."

A guidebook is propped open in her lap, notes scratched in the margin, things starred and underlined.

"Planning the Post-Suicide Deluxe Tour? " I ask.

She shuts it quickly, gripping it tight between her hands. *Greek Islands 2003.* Both current and specific. I try to imagine her wandering the travel aisle of some megabookstore, squatting before the Greece section. Sarah likes to arm herself with odd facts and statistics: heliotrope and honey. It is her way to make sense of what she does not yet know.

"Jack, let me be clear," she says. "I'm here to help you get through this, to manage with the getting around. But I'm not yours all the time. You know that, right? This is not save-our-marriage-through-shared-devastation-vacation. This doesn't make us not end."

Again, the bus dips into some foot-deep pothole and I wince. My leg aches as if I'd crabbed these miles bare-kneed on stones like a medieval penitent. Sarah relents, pats the top of her smooth knee.

I swing my leg over and prop it on hers. The muscles hang loose from my calf and thigh. Her fingers settle like birds where my bones and ligaments are anchored together by pins and screws. "It will be okay," she says, and taps a gentle rhythm. Then her hands, on second thought, fly suddenly away.

We both know it will not. Not for Kate. Not for me. For Sarah, yes.

I imagine that, in addition to the guidebook, there is also a journal she will fill with pressed flowers and neat columns of strange local specialties she will try once and once only (goat balls, sheep innards, unpronounceable unidentifiable grilled meats). In her suitcase, I can imagine a rubber-banded stash of index cards listing obscure Byzantine churches huddled in remote towns, their peeling frescoes and cracked icons, their collapsed barrel rooftops and empty windowpanes, swallows roosting on the crossbeams, shitting all over what is left of the impassive, sun-bleached Madonnas. And of course, she will jot off postcards, carefully worded—*Jack is doing as well as can be expected*. Which is to say, not okay.

My sister is dead, by her own hand. The administrator in Athens, Ms. Maria Nikolaides, a stern woman who mentioned that her B.A. was from some business college in Indiana, said that I did not have to come all the way to Greece for the body and a suitcase of papers and clothes. Greece was a modern country. An E.U. country. Greece could certainly handle the respectful and efficient transport of a body and a suitcase.

"After all," she said, "Greece is the E.U. industry standard in international waterway shipping!"

There were certain documents and authorizations needed before aforementioned body and effects could be released, but she would see that everything was handled with the utmost proficiency. "She's my sister," I said. "Her name is Kate. She's not a fucking body."

"Excuse me sir, but I'm reminding you I received my B.A. in Indiana at Lakeland Business Institute and I know such words so I'm pleasing you to not use such words."

There was silence.

"Of course, sir," she continued, "there are things better accomplished by a live person. But sir, I give you the E.U. promise and satisfaction that the body and the suitcase will arise at your doorstep in perfect condition."

The last time I saw Kate the live person arise: Kennedy Airport, Security Gate, her red hair cropped close to her skull, a blue jewel glinting in the side of her nose, a stiff leather backpack slung over her shoulders. I don't know what she had in there except, of course, her medications that I'd bought since I had the money and she had no insurance. Three hundred and sixty capsules, that, taken in sufficient quantity, stop a body's heart and brain, dreams and breath.

At twenty-seven, Kate was already exhausted and as she turned to wave, I thought there was something final and empty in her smile, though Greece and its promise of light and lightness still waited for her beyond that metal detector and the dour security agent, beyond the boorish pat-down she was subjected to due to the alarm she triggered. That finality in her smile is only my retrospective knowledge. But still, the alarm sounded, the wand whined as it passed back and forth over her body.

I should have called Kate back. That's what you do when you love someone, even when you're exhausted, even when they exhaust you. But I was relieved to see her go. Final blueprints were due on an eight-bedroom house in East Hampton for an unnecessarily wealthy young couple. I'd been stalling, drawing one tedious, rambling shingled cottage after another, concentrating my efforts on getting Sarah out of her sister's sixth floor walk-up, off the pull-out love seat, and back into our one-bedroom, doormanned, elevatored apartment. The couple was about to pull the project from the firm—they too were bored by what I'd been giving them, though that was what they initially wanted. So three days and nights on speed and no sleep equaled one clean, vacant, long windowed Philip Johnson rip-off and one swooning couple liberated from the Glen plaids and inherited pearls. I, however, was spent and stumbled over to the walk-up, determined to bring Sarah back home, to make it right between us again.

It was as simple as this: four flights up I tripped, fell all the way back down.

We arrive at Moutsouna in the late haze of dusk, the very last passengers on the bus, and are deposited at the entrance to the town square that sits on a sandy bay. It is as Kate described in one of her letters: three old men at the kafenio, spinning their koboloi, smoking, drinking coffee and ouzo. Blue doors. Pots of red geraniums. Cats. Too many cats winding their tails around chair legs, mewling over fish guts. And dogs splayed out under trees, wrecked from the heat, from too many puppies sucking their teats.

Sarah is at a loss. Her guidebook has not prepared her for this. There are no helpful women pointing the way, offering cold water and a bathroom. Only these old men eyeing her green shorts and my leg with suspicion. After all, the last foreigner through these parts may have been Kate, who'd gone and made an American mess of herself. And here we are with our matching red American Tourister suitcases, wedding presents that had traveled with us to Thailand, Italy, St. Lucia. After this final trip together we'd divide the pieces. Would she get the weekender, and I the garment bag? Would they ever meet unexpectedly on the tarmac, bump into each other on the baggage carousel? Hello former life, hello lost love. But here we are now, side by side. The cripple and his in-name-only-wife with their matched luggage. An American Spectacle.

It is rough going over the gravel and all eyes are on me, waiting to see if the crutches will skid out, if I'll land on my ass. Sarah holds her breath. She knows if I fall it will be days before I'll be able to get up again, and more murky days on Percocet. This is how close to the bone I am cutting it with this trip. But there was, is, no one else to come. Our parents are both long gone. I am the live person. I am the person who can arise. I am now, or soon will be, a family of one.

I stop short of the table, breathing hard already. "Excuse me," I say, to no one in particular. "Hello. Pension Anna?" I don't know if they will know English. I don't know Greek except what I'd found repeated in my sister's letters. I don't know what is rude or respectful here. So I decide to keep it short, keep my distance. Fewer words, fewer opportunities for misunderstanding.

All the men exhale at once. Are they the male fates knitting their smoke together in tacit agreement to send us in the wrong direction, to Hell? They are impenetrable and unperturbed.

"Pension Anna?" I say, trying a different inflection. Silence again. From inside the kafenio someone is shouting and techno music blares briefly from a radio, then it goes quiet, and something that I take to be Greek news comes on.

Sarah shouts out, "Please, Pension Anna?" She walks over to the table. The men startle and laugh, reveal yawning gaps where there should be teeth. The one in the middle reaches over and pats her hand.

"Anna," he says, and points left, down the road along the bay, then makes a snake-like motion with his hand and a clicking noise with his mouth. This can only mean far. Very far.

"Taxi?" Sarah asks, and points back to me. They all look again, appraising my leg, the crutches, the sheen of sweat on my face. I look away to the sea, back to our red suitcases so solemn and absurd in the middle of the dusty road. Construction cones. Bowling pins ready to be knocked down.

The men speak loudly, arguing perhaps, though what they say is unintelligible to us. They are deciding upon a course of action. Pick our pockets? Rape Sarah? Nothing seems impossible in this evening half-light.

Sarah waits, fists clenched at her side, exhausted by all of this negotiation. The man in the middle jumps up, disappears inside the kafenio, and returns with a young man, bare-chested and hairy, swinging a sharp knife. His hair is sheared and his nose juts sharply from his face giving the impression that he is all hard angles. A heavy gold cross hangs from his neck on a thick chain.

He wipes the knife across the seat of his jeans but doesn't offer to shake our hands. "Amerikanee eehsay? I am Nikos. I give you ride to Anna." His English is good, if halting. "Let me wash first. I clean the fish for tonight so I stink. Maybe you come and eat some like Katerina. You come for Katerina, nai? "

I shrug, uncertain. It is English but it means nothing. I glance at Sarah. Perhaps she caught something? But she is leaning against one of the rickety wooden chairs, eyes closed. A scrawny tabby circles her feet, mewing for scraps. Its orange tail, a strange lopped stump, twitches back and forth.

Nikos stamps his foot. "Ssshttt," he says. The cat streaks off, disappears beneath an overturned boat that is pulled up onto the beach. He looks away, then clears his voice and says again, "You come for Kate? Katerina? Kate? Katerina?" He reaches his hand out, forgetting that it is rank with fish, and rests it on Sarah's shoulder.

I startle. Her name is a flower unfolding again and again in his mouth. She sounds alive, waiting for us somewhere, sitting on a hot stone beach, flicking a fat ant from her shoulder, turning her face to the sun, her skin brown and freckled, spitting olive pits into the sea.

Sarah turns and is suddenly, momentarily surprised that the hand on her shoulder is not mine, but Nikos's. Her smile is at once filled with gratitude. She rests her hand on his.

He steps back, nods, and says he will wash up, that we must sit and have something to drink. Two tall glasses of cold water, two tall iced coffees, *frappes* he calls them, two small crescent cookies that taste of anise. The frappe is bitter and strong with at least three inches of thick foam floating on top. Sarah gulps her water in one long swallow, leaves the coffee, and walks the few yards down to the empty beach.

Dingy lounge chairs speckled in bird shit are stacked in four squat columns; umbrellas are piled in an enormous heap like a strange mass of red and white striped insects, wings tucked under, encrusted in salt. A fat gull skitters across the sand and hops up onto the overturned boat. It digs its long yellow beak furiously into gray feathers, ruffling up mites, then flaps its wings once and settles in, impassively surveying the scene. Does anyone pay his five Euros for the sun bed? Does anyone come here, to the end of the road?

Sarah kicks off her sneakers, shakes her hair free, and strides into the water. She reaches down, brings up handfuls of pebbles, and hurls them away. Further out, water laps her calves, thighs, then her green shorts. When she turns and waves, her hand brushing the sky, I know she is not asking me to hobble down and join her. She is merely checking in, making sure I haven't toppled from the rickety chair and brained myself on the stony patio. Before I can think to wave back, she is under water, swimming furiously, quickly away.

The gull gives no notice, though the old men are suddenly quiet.

When she surfaces, her hair hangs in dark skeins across her face.

It has been a long day and despite the guidebook, she loved Kate, took better care of her perhaps than me. Sarah had been the one to find the psychiatrist. Had been the one to check her into the hospital and check her back in again. When Kate stopped taking her medication for the tenth or twentieth time, when she said she was sure she was well, when she disappeared and finally called from some godforsaken rat-ass town in Florida without any money— asking for help?

At the time, my attention was tied up in a dark Lower East Side loft: another young moneyed couple wanted the place gutted down to its bones, reconceived into something fabulous, something shimmering, worthy of a spread in *Architectural Digest.* What that something fabulous was? Nobody yet knew, but it had to be fabulous and fast.

So Sarah was the one who went down to Ft. Lauderdale and found her holed up in a dank room in one of those awful trucker motels. Apparently she met some guy in a bar in the city; they were tired of all the gray slush, all the shit of New York, and so, she got in his car. They drove south, and when he got tired of her, he left. Sarah had been the one who had suggested the recuperative month in Greece, imagining an olive grove, peaches, blue sky, the buoyancy of salt, water, light. Elements not present in a New York City winter. A rest cure. So this trip, this task, this penance is difficult for her in ways I cannot know.

They load me into the bed of a pickup along with two sacks of potatoes, a box of onions, a case of water, four bottles of wine, and a stinky dog, Argos, with matted orange fur. Sarah tries to make me comfortable, but will not look me in the eye when she closes the truck-bed gate.

"I'm going to sit up front," she says, combing her fingers through her wet hair, catching them in the knots. "I'll try to keep him from going too fast. Nice and easy over the bumps." Her legs are marbled in dried salt, her shorts still wet.

The dog leans against my shoulder for the entire ride out. Every now and then he licks my ear. I scratch his head, feel little lumps that I take for ticks. He thumps his tail in appreciation. Suddenly, he vaults over the side of the truck and I watch him bound off down the beach, his enormous balls swinging against his hind legs. He is chasing some sort of stalky brown bird that he will never catch. The bird hops along the shoreline, teasing him, letting him get close, then quickly, legs up, skims the water's surface. The dog still runs, still follows. Such ease, those gangly legs, those joints in perfect hinged movement. It is beautiful to watch his failure.

I lean my head against the cab, feel the murmuring of their voices inside. What can they have to talk about? What can she understand?

Where is the octopus? The secret swimming cove? The ancient ruin?

I could tell her she need not look far. The ruin is here. Right here.

There was the first letter from Kate:
Jack,
Outside the village, there is this little house where I live on the beach with a pale green doorway fringed by the dark vines of grape leaves. Kyria Anna's home. In her garden, under the purple sweet of lilacs, a marble man sleeps. One of the kouroi of Naxos. 'He is old', she whispers to me, 'three thousand years old'. His fingers are worn by the wind. His nose is flattened by rain. His thighs, once full, are now thin. Kyria Anna whispers, afraid her voice might rouse his heavy stone lids, that the man might wake and discover his trouble. 'What trouble?' I ask. It seems a perfect place to sleep and sleep. She pulled back the low-lying limbs of the lilac. Those long-ago hands

*which had coaxed life from that marble had abandoned him,
left him without legs, left him to the unformed bone of marble.
Worn down now by countless seasons of mud and rain, by her
hands pruning lilacs, skimming his rigid hips. I fell by his side
and wept into my hands. What an unnatural, unbearable
sleep. Kyria Anna stroked my hair, understanding my grief.
This place is beautiful but I see too much here. Sarah would
understand the damage all this light can do.*

The dog is paddling in the sea now. I watch as Argos
disappears beneath the water then reappears again, paddles
in a circle, around and around, pawing like a child after
some errant beach ball, then back underwater, then he is out
of sight entirely. Fishing? Pleasure paddle? Or some trick
to relieve the ticks and the smear of rash across his belly?

Inexplicably, the dog gets there before we do, already
snoozing on the portico. Pension Anna is surrounded by
a rose-trellised garden that stretches out towards the beach
and nothing else. The hand-painted sign rocks in the breeze.
I smell salt, sea, roses, something cooking—meat, olive oil.
Nikos has gone on inside, carrying the sacks of food for his
mother. This is what Sarah has discovered: he lives behind
the kafenio, his kafenio, and his mother here.

"Jack," she says, "He knew Kate. She used to walk to
the kafenio every afternoon, all the way from here, and
drink retsina, and she would sit at the same little table and
cry. The old men called her crazy."

"He told you all this?"

"His English isn't as bad as you think. He has cousins
in Astoria who visit every summer. Let's get settled." She
hefts a bag on each shoulder and marches up the gravel
walk, determined to get on with our evening and the next
day.

It is stupid of course. I need never have left New York. I could have sent Francis X. Cleary Funeral Home to Kennedy Airport to collect Kate. I could have had her personal effects shipped to my apartment. Alternately, Sarah and I need never have moved beyond the air-conditioned splendor of the Hyatt Regency Athens. We could have dealt with Ms. Maria Nikolaides with her Indiana B.A., signed the papers in the hotel bar, gotten smashed on those iceless gin and tonics, then taken the elevator to our rooms on the eighth floor. Kate was already waiting for us at the Athens airport. She is still waiting for us there in cold storage. We are taking a three-day detour to see what she saw before she died.

What did Kate see here? There are no trees, no fragrant groves of olives or almonds. Only a desert meeting the blue sea, dunes sprouting scrub pine, prickly pear, a few fishing boats in the distance aimlessly drifting on glass.

"Germans," Kyria Anna, says later that evening when she comes to our room offering a tray of little plates of food: olives dressed in oregano and oil, sliced tomatoes, a hunk of feta, meatballs, bread, a small carafe of yeasty wine, a bowl of cherries. Argos waits in the doorway, whining. "That's why my husband built here. Nothing around. Nowhere. They come for sun and stay for summer. Germans don't like crowds or clothes, just their, how do you say," she points to her chest and arms, "their bodies cooking, and wrinkles, and titties to their knees." She laughs. "They come in three weeks." She ticks off the time on her fingers.

"But what do you think?" she continues. "Katerina say you build big houses in America. What do you think of what my husband build?"

"He did fine. This should stand the test of time," I say, though already I can feel the room is not level. This may be just a matter of the foundation sinking unevenly over time.

She looks at me slyly, then laughs. "You not see the cracks on the wall outside? Nikos is always fixing. You look tomorrow then you tell me what builder my husband is. He was a teacher first of mathematics. Not builder."

I can see why Kate liked her. She is a generous, direct woman, though dressed, as all the widows in Greece seem still to be, in black. Like a magpie, she chatters on, inspecting us, hovering in the room, adjusting the covers around the edges of the twin beds, counting the utensils and the pots and pans in the economical kitchenette, swatting a moth dead.

"Your sister," she finally says, and shakes her head, "she was too much alone. She was cursed with it. And you?" she says, tilting her head towards my leg.

"I fell," I say. "Far."

Sarah laughs.

Kyria Anna does, too. "Katerina say you fell to rock bottom. Now I see what she mean."

"I'm getting better," I say. "I won't need these forever." I send the crutches clattering to the floor.

"Kalinikta," Kyria Anna says, then she is gone, back out into the inscrutable night with all those stars.

We eat like two year olds, oil dripping down our chins, using our fingers. We have no napkins, just wipe with the backs of our hands, licking off the excess with our tongues. Laugh too much.

"She's lovely," I say, remembering her shuffled hop into the air, the fruitless clap of her hand for the moth, the way she wet her thumb and rubbed at some nonexistent stain on the whitewashed wall.

Sarah chews thoughtfully on bread, swallows. "When I was signing in, she was watching you through the window, one hand worrying a bit of lace she'd pulled from her pocket, the other rubbing at her eyes. She was crying I think."

"Kate liked to write about her. She said she made her feel safe."

Kyria Anna has the ugliest toes I've ever seen. Nails yellow and twisted, they poke through her black stockings that she wears even in the deadliest heat. Even when she's out back in her garden watering her endless rows of tomato plants. They are also the most beautiful toes I have ever seen.

We sleep soundly under the ticking of a fan, beside the wash of the tide even in our hard twin beds. We have arrived at Kate's end. It is no starting point. Our map divulges no roads, there are no penciled in x's, no hieroglyphs hinting some dirt path.

I dream not of my real fall, not my real fucked-up fall down all those flights of stairs, but a dream fall with Kate. (Oh Kate! My heart leaps. You are alive!) I dream of falling with Kate. Kate and I stumbling over rusty spikes of barbed wire. We slip suddenly down the loose shale of a bald cliff nettled with briar and thyme, tumble over the crumbling foundations of some long-forgotten house. The only sound is our slipping, rocks skidding and clacking, then nothing.

I wake to light through the cracks in the shutters, the sheet tangled around my legs. Across the room in the other narrow bed, Sarah's body is a graceful curve and dip under the sheet; it makes a steady rise and fall. I fall back sweating to the pillow, grateful that she is here. Olives and oregano are in my mouth, under my tongue. Our suitcases stand as we left them at attention against the wall. We never even bothered to unpack, to undress, to brush teeth, to speak, finally, of Kate. Two days to get on with it before returning to Athens.

Kyria Anna is singing while hanging the wash, a great tub of sheets and towels she wrings out by hand then clips up to the line. I find her out back, in her black dress, black stockings, and slippers. Already the laundry line holds twenty feet of voluminous white underwear and thick-strapped bras, dresses and housecoats and slips, though mostly what hangs there are clothes belonging to Nikos.

"*Kalimera*, Jack," she says. "You sleep good?"

"Good morning," I say and check my watch. Six-thirty.

"Katerina always up with the birds, too. Then fly with the birds into hills. She climb the big rocks." She turns and waves her hand in the direction of the hills which then give way to rock shears. "She go all day. I say take care. Dogs. Gypsies. They curse you. You get...how you say?" She twirls her finger in the air.

"Dizzy?" I say.

"Yes," she says, then points to her ankle. "She comes back one day and walk like this." She staggers down a row of tomatoes, dragging her foot along the ground, then stops, raises her hands in apology.

"It's okay," I say. "This isn't forever. What happened?"

"She not say. Her eye, her..." She points to her ankle.

"Ankle," I say.

"Ankle," she says. "Blood. It all big with blood. Maybe, she fall." She twists a towel and water spills to the ground. She looks at me, studies my face as I study hers, and nods. I know what she will say. "Maybe she jump off rock."

I walk the garden rows, the vines heavy with tomatoes, eggplant, and squash. How does anything grow here? I can't imagine rain. I lean on the crutches, study the rocks above the hills, and imagine Kate, eyes closed, taking one of her crazy leaps.

A pink-flowered bathing suit, zinc oxide smeared across her nose. I am dog-paddling in the deep end of the pool at Chequasset Country Club, embarrassed at babysitting my little sister while our parents play golf, but so be it. In revenge, I have dared her: "Jump off the high dive, Kate." She will do it. Really she has no choice. She climbs the ladder, her knobby legs shivering, and stands on the edge, contemplating the fall between the solid here of the pebbly board beneath her feet and the forever of below. "Chicken," I yell. And with that, she bends her knees and hurls herself, all flailing arms and legs into the air. Suddenly, I can see she is not ready for this, will belly flop, strike bottom, smack concrete. She will, I know with terrifying certainty, die.

I dive under. I cannot find her.

But she has already broken the surface, hooting and hollering, is climbing back up the ladder, and is on the edge of the diving board. "Kiss my ass, Jack," she shouts, then turns, points to her bottom and jumps in again, backwards this time.

Argos trots over, a mangled rabbit in his mouth. With a final regal shake, he dumps it at my feet. There is no blood, just the limp brown body, neck wrenched at the odd angle, dark eyes open, unblinking. He is panting, has given good chase, his breath hot and heavy on my leg. "Good boy," I say, though I am not at all sure of this. I scratch his head then look back up to the hills, the rocks, then the sky. What is it that writers and painters are always saying about Greece? The effects of light. The glorious effects of light. But the dangerous, delirious effects, too.

Last letter from Kate:
Jack:
I wander at will up here. If there are No Trespassing signs, I can't read them. It is quite literally all Greek to

*me. Besides, I long to trespass, to be where I shouldn't. I
won't lie and say I am well but I am at home with these
rocks and stars and sea. You would be, too, I think. I
wander at will up in the hills. I lay on rocks like some
pagan lolling about, watch ants in procession, stare down
the goats, keep my pockets weighted with stones to throw at
terrifying dogs. I found a little chapel. The door was open.
A Madonna with sad eyes hung next to altar. On the
floor, a box of thin beeswax candles and matches. I closed
the door and lit the candles one by one. One hundred,
two hundred? I lost count. I knelt and prayed, my knees
and feet numb, but I kept at it until all the candles burned
down to the quick, smoked out. How long was I there?
Hours, days, years? I pricked my finger on a thorn and left
a thumbprint of spiraled blood over the chapel door when
I left. Do you understand?*

Kate was not crazy. She didn't magic-marker walls
with miniscule letters; she didn't receive signals from aliens
through her silver fillings. She had an understandable,
controllable disease. That's what her doctors said. Bipolar
disorder. Completely manageable with the right cocktail
of drugs they assured, their black pens scratching notes on
her charts. Disorder equals disarray, muddle, unrest, chaos,
bedlam. But also suggesting its opposite. The mind's house
can be made orderly, restful, safe for habitation again.

I don't pretend to understand how Kate felt, either sick
or well. It was easier to love her when she was well than
sick. But that does not mean I loved her any less. That I
did not jump out of bed at three in the morning when she
called, her voice small and desperate: "Please, Jack. Please
help me." That I did not chase down the first empty cab,
running after it like a maniac, half-dressed, wild with fear

that my decision not to call someone else was the wrong decision.

It does not mean that I was not angry, unbearably angry at her for what she did to her thin arms and legs, her hollow stomach and tiny, sad breasts, those razor cuts, those cross-hatchings, all that blood. It does not mean that I did not turn and run into that ugly kitchen and puke into the sink full of dishes.

But Kate was my sister and I was her brother-knight charged with her safekeeping. I splashed my face with water, gargled, and walked back into that bedroom. I scooped her from the floor and stood with her in the shower in the bright fluorescent lights, sponging down all that damage. Nothing too deep, nothing that couldn't be butterfly bandaged, nothing that wouldn't eventually heal. Except what we both would always carry inside of us. Not her naked body and all that blood, not even the scars that would remain in thin, white splinters across her thighs, her arms, and stomach, but this: love is horrifying, holds us hostage, requires us always to answer the phone, to make the drive, to wash the blood from the body, to look at each other clearly under light and not flinch, not look away.

We eat yogurt, honey, and peaches for breakfast. Sarah reads the guidebook.

"You don't need that," I say. "There are ruins right here. An ancient statue out back that Kate wrote to me about. And up in the hills, some sort of chapel you can walk to in a few hours time. There's a Madonna icon, probably in disrepair."

She reaches across the table for my hand. It is unexpected. "I'm thinking I might stay on. Not here. But when we get back to Athens, if you're doing okay and think you can manage the flight back. I might try some other islands." Her voice trails off. She lets go of my hand and bites into a peach.

Is she looking at me or sideways to the sea, to another shore, another breakfast of peaches and honey with another man? Perhaps *Greek Islands 2003* has been annotated beyond Naxos since our flight over. Where might a soon-to-be-single, thirty-something woman go? Her dark sunglasses make her impenetrable this morning, something maybe she finds necessary, since we haven't shared a bedroom in over a year. Such close proximity to the past, to love that is over, is disturbing, upending the fragile balance of days and nights.

"Do what you want," I say. "We're under no obligation to each other anymore." Who is this person sitting here? Who can think about island hopping when there is still Kate, still all these strangers who speak her name, and summon her up out of this bright and empty sky?

She wipes her mouth with the back of her hand. "There are monasteries and churches all over the place, and so much in deterioration, so much in need of help. I might be able to get some research done. I might even do some good while I'm here."

Sarah stands, braces herself against the iron railing, and hocks the peach pit from her mouth. It clatters, like a stone, against the concrete walk. She says, "Because all I can do now is think that this is the place where Kate killed herself. Right here. Maybe in my bed, maybe in yours. And we did nothing to stop her. We just packed her off to die alone."

How do we do good here?

It is late morning. We make our way down the path behind the pension towards the kouroi, Kate's sleeping statue. I shuffle behind Sarah and Kyria Anna, amused by their aimless chatter, their wandering back and forth across the path as Kyria Anna points to this and that flower, rattling off a fast string of Greek names. Sarah nods, tries to pronounce what is unpronounceable on a first try. Every few minutes we pause, wipe dust from our eyes with a damp lace-edged handkerchief. Suddenly we stop beneath an olive tree, swapping swigs of water from a plastic jug. Kyria Anna sits on the ground, stretches her legs out, and kicks off her slippers. Sarah plucks a red poppy and tucks it behind her ear. I rest my crutches against the tree, lean into the trunk, look up through the silvery green leaves to the sky. Around us, shrill cicadas.

Kyria Anna wags her finger. "I not show him to everyone. Not to the Germans and their titties," she says. "Not to Greeks. Not to government. You show, you lose. Too many tourists. No quiet then. Then I become bus stop." She points over a little rise. "He is there. Over the stone wall. Behind the trees. Lemons. Lilacs. He is there. You go. I stay and sleep a little." She scuttles up against the trunk and closes her eyes. Her toes, I notice, poke through her stockings. They are ugly, beautiful.

I can't climb over a four-foot stone wall and Sarah can't hoist me over. What more would I need to see anyway? Kate showed him to me. Sarah fills in the gaps and comes running back, her hands filled with lilac bundles, pockets crammed with lemons, three bee stings on her thigh. She is yelping.

"What did you do?" I ask. "Pilfer the treasury and fuck the god?"

"Shut up," she says. "Just help me over."

Kyria Anna mixes up a mud paste and spreads it on the three swollen lumps. Sarah sighs. Kate would not have been pleased at such ransacking of her marble man, though I am at such a thought: Sarah tramping up over the block of marble, snapping off the lilac branches, shaking the lemon tree, satisfied only when she hears the thump of lemons hitting him squarely in the face. What use is he to her, this half-finished man, this lump of marble, this legless thing? Did she straddle him, spit in his face, make him eat crow?

Nikos has come to take us for a swim. I point stupidly to my leg, as if he hasn't noticed.

He smiles. "It's okay. Water is flat where we go. No waves. You sit. It will be good for the leg. You see."

Is he even a day over twenty five? Maybe he just looks young, with that chest, those arms and those barrel legs that lift sacks of potatoes, that heave wheelbarrows of cement up the gravel drive to Kyria Anna's expanding patio, that can, I imagine, flip a woman onto her back, make her sigh with pleasure. He has brought three masks, two snorkels, and one float. He and Sarah will hunt octopus while I bob around. He says he can catch an octopus with his hands and a piece of stocking.

"What do you mean 'stocking'?" I say.

"You know," Sarah says, "panty hose." Apparently something else they found to talk about in the tiny cab of the pickup.

Once again, I am propped up in the bed of the pickup with Argos who curls up next to my feet, head on my crutches, and sleeps. In order to get to the cove, we head inland, pass fields of truck-sized rocks, then fields of recently harvested potatoes heaped in piles like collections of shrunken heads. And pens of goats, always goats with little crumbling goat-herder's huts. No level used to build these. Just stones and mud, a bit of straw and dung, a good eye and necessity. Like a monk's cell. Something Kate would have liked, too. The narrow bed, the square table beneath the window, the stone jug filled with cold water, the hard bread and sharp cheese, the trill of birds, the warm flood of light through the window.

Our hermit's camp we'd built one summer was nothing more than a piece of plywood and tarp stocked with a cooler of Coke and peanut butter sandwiches. Our parents were divorcing. Not, I should add, amicably. Our father had become an extraordinary drunk; once he showed up at the house, waving around his hunting rifle, threatening to kill us all. My mother was off on the golf course, in her pink seersucker shorts. They were monstrous. So Kate and I hid out in our hermit's camp in the woods just beyond the neat fencing of our suburban development with our stockpile of books, our ammo of candy bars, in our platoon of two.

When does it sour? When does the bleating of the goats sound like betrayal? When does the morning sun begin to burn? I rub my knees, shift weight, ease the pressure, though nothing seems to work. Argos woofs in companionable complaint. I pull my cap over my eyes, try to sleep.

The cove is beautiful. We are standing at the side of the road looking down the narrow dirt path into the water. The only way down. It is the fall from my dream. Nikos looks stupid and uncomfortable. Obviously, he forgot about the descent. Sarah stands there chewing her lip, twisting the ties of her sarong. Argos, fleet-footed, is already down the path, barking at us from below. I can tell from the way his paws kick up the ground that it is not sand, but a beach made of pebbles, brilliant white in this blaze of sun. Above, the fat bees circle us, buzz our ears, then dive into tall red flowers, lapping nectar; they emerge dusty and incandescent. No one speaks. There is only Argos's desperate bark and the endless hum of the heat.

"Fuck it," I say. "We came all the way out here. You'll just have to carry me."

I can see this surprises Sarah. Nikos, who does not know me, does not know to be surprised. He squats. "Get on," he says, and I hug my arms around his neck. We proceed carefully, too carefully I want to say to him, as we are never in any danger of slipping. His balance is perfect. He could balance an elephant, a tiger, and ten acrobats on his back or a jumble of five sons and daughters. Every now and then I swing my head around to look at Sarah whose lips are curled back in the flat smile of fear. The snorkel gear hangs around her neck and plastic lunch bags dangle from each hand like weights. Her body jogs forward and backward, heels skidding out under her, sending bits and pieces of cliff our way. She is afraid for me and watches for the tiny rocks and sticks that threaten Nikos's way, my way, forgetting to watch her own. More than once she swears.

At the bottom Nikos wants to run back up to fetch my crutches. It is pointless, I tell him. They'll just sink right in. Before he can argue, my tee shirt and sandals are off and I am already crab-crawling in the water, Argos close behind, his nose bumping my head, mistaking me for kin. I don't mind.

When I turn back, Sarah is shaking her head, laughing, and if she is shocked, refuses to show it because she has stripped off her bikini top. A challenge. Briefly, I look away. What is the etiquette of divorce, even one proceeding as amicably as ours? When your soon-to-be-ex-wife is standing half-naked before you, do you look away? And when you look back, how long can you look? Can you, dare you, resurrect the memory of what once was? Her breasts against your chest, in your hands, in your mouth? When I look back, Sara's breasts are a thick smear of white sunscreen. Her thighs show the red welts of the bees.

Nikos tosses her the tins of anchovies and dolmades from the plastic bag. "Wind," he says, "put it on top of the clothes." He blows up the float and brings it to me, then points towards the far end of the cove, a half mile or so away. "We'll swim out. But you use this," he says, and hands me a mask. "Just hang head over into water, and you will have good morning. Be happy." He smiles, spits in the mask then dunks it under water. "That's what I say to Katerina. Be happy." He rubs the mask clean with his fingers, pulls it down over his eyes, and hands it over. "There. You see good now. Twenty twenty. Argos will stay for companion. Just be careful of urchins. If you are so lucky to step on one, you must pee on you."

"Nikos," I say, "I can't step on one. I can't walk. I could only fall on one. Which would mean I'd had an accident. And you mean unlucky. Not lucky."

"Unlucky, yes." He waves his hands. "Do not say accident. You will be fine. But is good to know in case you step on urchin. You pee on you." He holds an imaginary and extraordinarily large penis in his hands and pretends to pee on the bottom of his foot that he has raised into the air. He jumps up and down, shouting, "Ouch! Ouch! Ouch!" He glances over at Sarah to see if she is watching this idiotic bit of pantomime.

She is and is laughing but then suddenly is worried. "You won't go out far, will you, Jack? Not so deep that you can't sit up if you fall?" She jams a water bottle down into the rocks beside me, under water, to keep it cool and close.

"I'm not some invalid. Go," I order. "Kiddie pool, water wings, and Argos the Lifeguard. What else could I need?"

They cast their bodies, bellies down, into the water, skimming across it like skipped stones. I reach for Sarah's foot, not to stop her, just to tell her to be careful, but she shimmers away. For several minutes I watch the pair of orange snorkel tubes pushing through the surface like periscopes. If only I could see what is happening beneath: toe striking thigh, hand grazing nipple, breath quickening. Then the surface is unbearably still, and they move discreetly, proficiently, feet churning like waterwheels, hunting their octopus.

Argos paddles in, trots to shore, and ceremoniously licks my knees. I pour out handfuls of water from the bottle. He laps gratefully then retreats to the shade of a rocky overhang, collapsing into sleep.

What is there to see in all this blue? The cheap plastic mask puddles water, obscures vision. Hollowed rocks become ancient cups; corroded cans become bronze figurines. I am startled to realize that indeed I am looking for fossils, for shards of amphora, bits of pottery, that I am not just bobbing about in the sea, but hunting, too. In the shallows, the stony floor spills a prism of sedimentary colors: gold, copper, obsidian. Further out, along the rocky edges of the cove, sea urchins flower in prickly colonies. One false move and a spiny blossom could snap off. I tense, grip the edges of the float. My body is ill-suited for such delicate maneuvering, kicking as I can only with my one leg. I back paddle, steering the bulky float away from the rocks, from bumping into anything that might prick a hole.

Cautiously, I roll to my back, dangle my legs in the water, shut my eyes to the sun. There is no shutting out the sun though; it swims against my eyelids, itches against the salt on my skin. I doze. Five minutes? A half hour? The float doesn't seem to move, though suddenly I am beached and there is an old man standing above me, chattering at me, and I am waving my hands at him. What am I supposed to say?

"No, no Greek. English," I say, groggy with sun and sleep. Argos is at my side, barking. In warning? I don't know how to read him yet.

The man stops his chatter, smiles. He is holding baskets in each hand and squats down.

I sit up, swing my legs out in front of me. I would like to stand, but can't. I would like to explain this to him, but can't. So I just sit there like some dumb lazy American, some polio victim. Obviously, he is going to show me what he has in his baskets. Shrunken heads? I think of those mounds of potatoes. Bloody goat balls? He pulls back a cloth. Something white, spongy. Brain? I've never seen intestines, but maybe that.

"Tiree," he says.

I try a friendly shrug.

He pulls a knife from his pockets, dunks it in the water, carves off a piece of whatever it is and hands it over to me. Seeing as how there is no way to refuse, I eat.

Cheese.

He wants me to buy his cheese. I turn the pockets of my swimsuit inside out. I have no money. This time he shrugs, pats my head. "Okay," he tries. He takes out the round of cheese, wraps it in paper and sets it beside me. "Yassas," he says, and heads back up the cliff, whistling the whole way, though I can see it strains his muscles. The angle is steep. Rocks tumble, bounce back down to the bottom.

I unwrap the cheese, break off two hunks. One for Argos, one for me. Damn you, Kate. How could you leave all this?

They return triumphant. Nikos has an octopus crammed down inside the stocking that he has tied around his wrist. Sarah is exuberant. She tells me he has turned its head inside out.

"We grill octopus for goodbye dinner tonight," Nikos says.

She ties her bikini top back on, then joins me at the edge of the sea. We watch Nikos as he scrubs, then smashes the octopus against the rocks.

I point to the path. "I know Nikos is strong, but that path is harder going up. I watched someone do it."

Her hand is on my knee. "I won't let him drop you," she says.

Kyria Anna hangs the octopus on the laundry line to dry. "You look good," she says. "Better with sun. Maybe you stay?"

Is this how Kate succumbed? One month that became two, then three, then forever?

She pins up another tentacle. "You think of your sister. You not cursed like her. You sad. Your sister dead. Your leg not right. You get over it. But Katerina? She sad always. Morning and night. She cry into the yogurt. She cry into the sea. She cry for fleas on Argos."

I unpin the towels from the line. They are dry, stiff, sun-baked. Kyria Anna swats me away.

"Tst. Tst," she scolds.

"Let me help," I say. "I need something to do." I am close to tears. I could not save my sister. Nothing I could do could save my sister. I had my apartment, emptied of Sarah, a living-room couch, books and companionship, enough room. Both of us had been hobbled in some way, leveled by what life had thrown, what we had been unable to bear. But I sent her away to a beautiful, lonely place to die. The rest cure that was no hermit's camp, no bunker of two.

Kyria Anna must see something of this in my face. She hands over the laundry basket.

Sarah and I rest under the ticking of the fan. We have eaten with Kyria Anna and Nikos. Grilled octopus in lemon and oregano, meatballs, potatoes, tomatoes still warm from the sun, and wine that tastes of this soil. We leave for the port tomorrow afternoon. Nikos has offered to drive us. The bed of the truck over the stop-and-go of the bus. An easy choice. He will set up a mattress for me and, of course, Argos will be my faithful companion. Nikos promises, even at a careful pace, the ride will be much more efficient. Two and one half hours versus the six it takes the bus.

I have, I think, made my peace with Kate here, seen most of what she would have wanted me to see.

"Sarah, can I ask you something?"

She turns over, waiting.

"Would you try to find that chapel tomorrow? I'm sure Nikos would know where it is. He'd walk with you."

She breathes out. "That's it?"

"What else is there?"

"I don't want to sleep with him, Jack. You know, don't you?"

"Know what?"

"He was sleeping with Kate. He was in a sort of love with her. He found her and she was still alive. At least I think that's what he said. But you know, it's a big island, and the nearest hospital is so far away, and he didn't know what pills she'd taken, and he made it to the hospital, to the port in an hour and a half. At night, Jack. Just think, at night, in that goddamn truck, with Kate lying in the back, Kyria Anna holding on to her and the truck for dear life, and who knows, Argos probably back there too, all of them praying, and Nikos speeding on these fucking roads in the middle of the night. Or maybe he just thought she was still alive. He loved her, so maybe he was just hoping he felt something at her throat jump against his hand."

I am listening to Sarah say this, listening to her voice rise and rise, and I know that Kate was dead by the time Nikos and Kyria Anna found her. Kate jumping off the high dive. She'd vault herself wholeheartedly into that forever. Damn her for almost killing those who loved her, for those who would vault themselves down dark, mountain roads, who would hold her body to theirs, whispering prayers, who would perhaps lick her feet, her ear, in search of some response.

And what would Sarah and Nikos find, what would anyone find up at that chapel? The nubs of candles? Melted puddles of beeswax? A rusty stain above the chapel door? Gone probably, or soon would be. As we will be. Though for now, we stay, hunt octopus and hang it out to dry in the glorious sun. Or tour another island, meet someone new, save a painting from the ravages of light. Learn how to walk again, how to swim in the salty sea. Dream of birds and rabbits, of a world without ticks and rashes, wake only to stretch and bark and run.

EGGS

Naturally, Noah and I had been trying to have a baby for a year: taking my basal body temperature each morning, at five A.M., conscientiously making love three times a day during prime ovulatory time, figuring out the physics of acrobatic positions and spermal flow. Latitude and longitude. Tilt pelvis forty-five degrees, align with the earth's axis, factor in rotational pull. This wasn't always easy. Sometimes we were tired or sick or just plain bored. Now insert penis, raise hips, thrust. All entrée, no appetizer.

Initially, we treated our ovulatory allegiance as an opportunity for exploration, playing strip poker, strip Trivial Pursuit, strip Go Fish; tying each other up; reading Penthouse Forum out loud; playing doctor. Once, we both had the flu, and after a flaccid love-making session we raced to the bathroom. I puked into the toilet, semen dribbling down my thighs, Noah in the sink, his penis quickly shrinking back to size.

And all those wasted dipsticks. I bought home pregnancy kits by the dozen. Despite the small window of ovulation and against all that we'd learned, every time Noah and I waited: he sat on the rim of the tub, counting down the minutes on his watch; I sat on the toilet re-reading again and again the color code for positive, the color code for negative, wondering if I'd been mixing them up. And every time, I sat on the toilet and tried not to cry as Noah took the dipstick from my hand, squinted at the color bar, shook it as if it were a thermometer and he could change the reading. "It's okay, Annie. Next time," he'd say, "just concentrate on the next time." Then I'd take it back, hold it to the awful light, trying to see in that dried splash of urine the failure of our cells to combine.

So we made an appointment with Doctor Shinefeld, Reproductive Endocrinologist. He was a burly Texan with a handlebar mustache that he swizzled between his fingertips. Two weeks out of each month he flew to his New York clinic, spending approximately ten minutes with each patient-couple. Our first visit, purely introductory, lasted eleven minutes and fifteen seconds.

"How often do you have sex?" he fired.

"Every day," Noah said, his palm smoothing down the seam of his khaki slacks.

"Three times a day during ovulation," I corrected.

Dr. Shinefeld laughed and pushed his black leather chair from side-to-side. "That bad?"

"Not that bad," Noah said.

"Yes it is," I said. "Why lie?"

"It's exhausting," Dr. Shinefeld counseled, "but I'm here to tell you you're not alone. This is a solvable problem for sixty-five percent of my patients. Sixty-five percent is pretty damn good."

I bobbed my head up and down, my smile wide and hopeful. Us! Us! Us! Saved! Saved! Saved!

Noah looked up. "But no hope for the other thirty-five percent."

Could I burn holes into Noah's head with the power of my glare? He refused to look my way.

Dr. Shinefeld dismissed the statement with a wave of our chart, which he then skimmed, his finger darting back and forth across the page. He stood up.

"Noah, it's Noah, right? Two-by-two and the ark? So that's something. Noah was the kingpin of reproduction, so take heart."

He sat back down and smacked his hand against the desk. "You've been playing a game of chance, you two. I know how hard it's been, but I'm about to load the dice."

He studied our chart again. "Now, Annie, since you're in the middle of your cycle, we'll have to wait a few weeks before we can do anything." He handed Noah a plastic cup and a lid. "If you can, then do, and we can start running tests on your sperm. And neatly please."

Dr. Shinefeld shook on his promise to help. "Wait here," he said, gave an encouraging pat to Noah on the back, and ducked out the door. We waited in the office.

This gave us time to study the Shinefeld gallery. One wall lined with degrees and awards. Another with a floor-to-ceiling corkboard crammed with hundreds of snapshots of babies galore. On his desk, a family photo in a gleaming silver frame: Dr. Shinefeld surrounded by a beautiful blond wife and seven children, toddler to teen, on a wide green lawn in front of an enormous white pillared house.

"Good advertising," Noah said, juggling the cup between his hands. "Not only has he fathered his own team, but all of New York City as well. Catch," he said, tossing the cup at me. "A Hail-Mary pass."

I chucked it back. "But you feel better about it, don't you?"

A nurse opened the door. "Sample time, Mr. Miles," she said. Noah tucked the cup into the crook of his arm and disappeared.

Later when he returned, minus the cup, I asked, "Any interesting ejaculatory aids in there?" Couldn't he have just been poked and prodded as I would be, the semen clinically suctioned out?

He shrugged. "It was a bathroom. Toilet. Sink. Utilitarian porn. A sign instructing me to wash my hands before and after sample collection."

Although Catholic, my parents did not believe in miraculous conception. In our extended family, it was as common and predictable as the miracle of transubstantiation at daily Mass. A messy event, its roots often traced to drunken Christmas and New Year's Eves, Saint Patrick's Day pub parties, Superbowl Sundays. My parents, Sheila and Paddy, joke that for each conception, a vicious hangover followed, which I firmly believe, since the only time I ever saw them possessed with lusty abandon—Dad sloppy kissing Mom's neck, solidly smacking her behind, Mom reeling Dad in with her opera-length pearls, tugging him up the stairs behind her like a panting dog—was when they had a few too many. Outside of that, my parents are a rather restrained couple.

Three children. All girls. Mathematically speaking, my parents were a couple blessed with the X chromosome. I was first. Four years later, Lizzie, two months early, was incubated until her lungs matured, so that by the time I was able to see her, she was already six weeks old and screamed so loud, I could hear her from inside Mom's greenhouse. Then JoJo, five years after Lizzie, popped out in the ambulance on the way to the hospital, and now can claim Exit Ramp 36 of the Long Island Expressway as her place of birth.

At three A.M., Lizzie called, drunk, her husband Kevin carrying on in the background.

"Annie," she moaned. "Annie Annie Annie Annie."

Let me get one thing straight. Lizzie does not get drunk. She does not ingest anything that might create caloric imbalance. Fat grams burned off at the gym, six mornings a week at six A.M.. And where was Kevin yelling from? He wasn't near the phone. His voice, decidedly sober, sounded far away. In the kitchen clutching a butcher knife? Out on Fifty-Second Street, swinging from the fire escape? Kevin was not a man to allow emotion to outweigh reason. He was a fastidious investment banker whose only whimsy was a silver golf-club tie clip affixed to an immaculately pressed gray suit.

Noah stuffed his head under the pillow. "Who is it?"

"Lizzie. It's okay. Go to sleep."

"She couldn't wait until a decent hour? Doesn't she think about what she might be interrupting?" He turned on his stomach, then side, then back again.

"We were asleep."

"My point exactly."

I slid off the bed and lay down on top of the green carpet that itched through my nightgown. Daisy, our golden retriever, always a glutton for sleep-space and Noah's warm body, yawned and wiggled from the foot of the bed into my vacancy. Again from the phone, "Annie Annie Annie Annie."

Was Lizzie lying down on the hardwood floor, empty six pack at her side? Or sitting at her desk, silk kimono cascading from her shoulders, martini in hand?

"Where are you?"

"Bathroom," she slurred. "I locked Kevin out."

Probably slumped on her cushioned toilet, portable phone hooked beneath her chin, wine bottle on the floor.

"You're drunk."

"I don't care." She held the phone away from her mouth and yelled, "Do you hear me, Kevin? I don't care if I vomit all over the bathroom and you have to clean it up." Poor Kevin. Red wine and pristine white tiles, white grout.

"Don't you have to work tomorrow?" No answer. "Were you fired, Lizzie, was that what happened?"

"Do I have to spell it out? Preg-nant."

I caught my breath in my throat. One one thousand. Two one thousand. Three one thousand. This is not you, this is Lizzie. Not you. Lizzie.

Lizzie fumbled with the phone, knocking it against the tiles. "Kevin's been poking holes in the condoms."

"He wouldn't do that."

"What, then? Super sperm that can swim through latex? He wants me pregnant. Barefoot and pregnant like some Irish Catholic hootchie-mama. You don't know Kevin when it comes to babies. He probably has a list of names already—Kevin Junior, Kevina, Kevonne."

"I'm sure this is just one of those things. It happens all the time."

"What would you know about it with your dog and your house and your perfectly arranged life?"

Deep breath in, then out. I rolled to my stomach, threw my arm over my head, held the phone close. Don't tell her anything. Your emptiness is not hers.

She laughed. "And then it'll be ten kids and my uterus will be dangling to my knees like Great Aunt Jean's. Screw Kevin and his goo-goo shit over the fetus. That's what I'm calling it. No attachments. Non-negotiable." She hung up.

The street lamp glowed against the shades. I waited, expecting the phone to twitch in my hand and ring and it would be Lizzie. She would have changed her mind; she would congratulate me on becoming an aunt, and ask if maybe Kevonne weren't really such a bad name after all.

"Annie, come back to bed."

Noah settled Daisy again at the bottom of the bed, rolled to the edge of the mattress, propped himself up on his side and patted the empty space.

I sat up, and even though I had been stretched out, felt stiff, smashed.

"She's pregnant," I said, and pressed my eyes into bent knees, trying to blot out the tears with their bony bumps. It didn't work.

Noah got out of bed, wrapped the comforter around our shoulders, and pulled me to his chest. I pushed away from him.

He reached for his glasses on the night stand and slipped them on, an attempt to look serious in his nakedness. He said, "Annie, this is not about you. Or us. Only Lizzie. Can you try to remember that?"

Blossoms, my flower shop, is located on Heights Road, in Pine Hills, sandwiched between Red Wagon Antiques and Keating Realty, across from R & J Candystore and Villa Pirelli's Pizzeria. JoJo, the artist of the family, painted the sign: *Blossoms* is written in a garland of daisies, lilies, roses, and sunflowers.

We grew up in this town on Overbrook Lane in a large white colonial, in-ground pool in the backyard and three new Cadillacs parked in the driveway each year: one for Dad, one for Mom, and one for the family. My father's dealership was only a few miles away, so Dad drove home each afternoon for lunch. Mom drove home from the botanical gardens where she volunteered or came in from her own with an armful of clippings she arranged in vases around the house. If it was summer, I was usually with Mom in the greenhouse or watching JoJo by the pool; Lizzie was usually with Dad at the dealership pretending to sell cars to her dolls. We would sit around the table eating tuna sandwiches and potato chips. If it was winter, then we were in the Holy Redeemer Girl's School cafeteria, lunching on lukewarm milk, bologna, peanut butter, or cheese sandwiches, wondering if Mom and Dad missed us and what exactly they would talk about without us.

We were a true family. Our parents took us everywhere with them, from dinners at fancy restaurants in the city to golfing vacations on Hilton Head, from suit shopping for Dad to manicures for Mom. Although our parents were a social couple—lots of friends, golf and tennis partners, business acquaintances—we, the sisters, were not. We had each other and moved together as a triumvirate. Lizzie and I even fought over JoJo: who got to pick out her clothes, who got to give her baths, rock her to sleep at night. We compromised: I got her on the even days, Lizzie on the odd. My mother says that the only thing we left her with was breast feeding, though I remember hugging JoJo to my flat chest, squeezing a bud of a nipple between my thumb and forefinger in an effort to pop it out, stiff and round, like my mother's.

I fell in love with flowers, the growing, cross-breeding, cutting, arranging, the quiet satisfaction, because of my mother. She used to let me help her in the greenhouse on weekends, after school, sometimes even into the late hours of the night when she chose to work under the dim light of the moon instead of fluorescence and heat lamps. The greenhouse stretched the length of the back fence, fifty feet long, twenty feet wide. It was a second home. The temperature, a constant seventy-eight degrees, was warm enough so that in winter we had Kentucky Fried Chicken picnics, dressed in shorts and tee-shirts, spread beneath the swooping leaves of elephant ears. In the summer, Mom and I worked in bikinis that she had especially made by Mrs. Vincinelli, the seamstress in town. Each winter Mrs. Vincinelli cut up Mom's old Lily Pulitzer dresses and sewed them into halter tops and flared-skirt bikini bottoms which Mom presented on the first day of spring, creating a routine that ushered in another season of expected, satisfying companionship and propagation.

At first, we spoke only of flowers as we transplanted baby shoots into their own pots, inspected the undersides of leaves for aphids and fungus, carefully sheared cut flowers for a bouquet. Mom used these early morning hours or late nights to explain the intricacies of propagation and reproduction, alluding that one could understand where babies came from by substituting certain floral attributes— stamen, ovary, stigma, sepal, petal, pistil—for their human counterparts. Later, we worked quietly, efficiently, professionally, until break time, where we sat in wicker chairs and sipped lemonade and talked of boys and proms and college plans and my sisters.

It seems as if there was always a playpen in the corner, always JoJo, curled up with a blanket and stuffed bear, gumming a fist in her mouth or waddling around the tables of flats, snatching buds, tearing petals, shoving bits of flowers in her mouth. I was indignant at her callous treatment, Mom indulgent, reminding me that I once ruined an entire flat of prized tulips when I stomped them in a tantrum.

Lizzie was not interested in flowers, complained they were boring, that the greenhouse made her mad and itchy with sweat, and went with Dad to the dealership, or swam

laps in the pool, or went to day camp and brought home
tennis trophies, macramé bracelets, and first-place riding
ribbons.

One late August afternoon during my senior year of
high school, as we repotted purple and yellow mums in
gray stone containers that would line the front steps, I told
my mother that I wanted to apply to Cornell's horticulture
program.

She balked, and without looking up, wiped the trowel
across her smock, front to back, in slow sweeping motions.
"Don't be stupid, Annie. You can't do anything with a
degree in horticulture."

I stabbed my trowel into a pot of mums, snapping off a
cluster of buds.

She tucked the broken stem into a pocket. "You'll be
a lawyer. A doctor. Not a gardener," she said, and slid
a wooden stake behind a stalk of drooping tomato plants,
twisted green wire around the stems, securing them firmly
to the crutch. She stood back to survey the morning's
work, brushed her hair back with the heel of her palm,
inadvertently streaking her forehead with soil. "Remember,
I don't have to make a living at it."

I stayed in Pine Hills, not, as my mother well knew,
because of my salary. Noah traded futures on Wall Street,
had a knack for it, which bought us a four bedroom Tudor
on Maple Ridge Road, and although we didn't have room
for a pool, Noah built a greenhouse off the sun porch where
I experimented with tulips, crossing hybrids for hardiness,
longer blooming cycles, shapelier leaves, perfect colors:
a true vermilion, peacock, or plum. You could say the
flower shop was my profession, the growing my passion, but
that wouldn't be true; I got to love the routine, puttering
around the cooler, choosing appropriate wedding bouquets,

designing a Get Well basket. Weekday mornings, I dropped Noah off at the Long Island Railroad station, and waited for the delivery truck that drove in from College Point with the week's buckets of blooms. I swept the floor, filled standing orders from restaurants, churches, private residences whose front hallways were festooned with fresh bouquets of my choosing, and waited for orders to come in from Pine Hills, the city, and the FTD link-up, orders from California, New Jersey, Florida, from Europe and Japan, from husbands on business trips feeling lonely or guilty or sometimes in love.

The morning after Lizzie's phone call, I began the day as usual, checked on the tulips, plucked dead leaves, watered the flats of seedlings, measured and penciled calculations into the growth chart. As morning broke and the sun began to warm the windowpanes, I waited for Noah to bring out coffee and bagels. We would sit on the low, wooden bench, collecting ourselves before we separated and went about the business of work.

By a quarter to seven, I'd waited long enough and went inside the house. Noah sat at the kitchen table, scanning the pages of the *Times*, his coffee in a plastic travel mug. He glanced up, eyes tired from a night of broken sleep. But I was tired, too.

"You know this is stupid," he said. "I don't even really know what you're angry about. At Lizzie for getting pregnant? Or at me for not getting you pregnant?"

"You'll be late," I said, poured coffee, and stalked out to the car. Noah followed, paper rolled up in one hand, briefcase in the other. We drove to the station in silence, listening to the news, careful to keep to our own sides of the car: Noah's hands in his lap; my elbows tight at my sides, fingers laced around the steering wheel.

Waiting for a light, we got stuck behind a minivan packed with a carpool of kids and a mother swatting at the child seated behind her. Before the light changed green, she hit the gas and tore through the intersection. "Watch the fucking light, idiot," I yelled

Noah glanced at me, eyebrows raised; his fingers brushed the back of my neck. "Take it easy, Annie, she didn't do anything to you."

I shrugged him off. "She could kill someone. Shouldn't she know that?"

I couldn't just be Lizzie's sister.

I bypassed the cluttered buckets of purple, blue, and pink carnations, and reached instead for the white roses, clipping their stems, tucking them in water vials. Even as I tied on pink and blue plastic rattles with curling ribbon, even as I sat a teddy bear in the middle of the flowers, I regretted it, but sent it anyway with a driver whose usual territory stretched from Great Neck to Sea Cliff, fifteen miles along a lip of the Sound, but to whom I paid an extra hundred bucks for the favor: *Rush Delivery*, Elizabeth McKay, Esq., Casey, Hawkins and Stephens, Attorneys at Law, 1450 Madison Avenue, Suite 2501.

An hour and a half later, in the middle of an FTD friendship mug, the phone rang.

"Bitch," Lizzie said.

I was curling silver ribbons that streamed from the #1 Friend balloon. "I'm sorry," I said. "I just thought that if you slept on it, if you saw how wonderful it could be."

"This is wonderful? Now I have to go up to every goddamn person in the office and explain that my sister thought she could talk me out of an abortion, bless her big heart, by sending flowers, but that she was mistaken and I won't need that maternity leave after all because as of next month, I will no longer be pregnant."

Her heels clacked along what I assumed was the floor of a long, empty hallway. Of course, she would still be as lithe and thin as ever, her black suit jacket buttoned snugly at her narrow waist.

"So in three weeks," she continued, "what you're going to do is send a nice somber bouquet, a tasteful card attached that offers condolences for the unfortunate miscarriage."

"I can't do that."

"You handle funerals."

"People don't send flowers for this."

"Well, as I'll explain, my sister has no tact or consideration. Which is why we aren't speaking anymore."

And we weren't.

For weeks after that first appointment with Doctor Shinefeld, Noah and I clung to his words, repeating them back and forth in the car, over dinner, before going to sleep, as if that ritual alone would get me pregnant. Sixty-five percent success. Sixty-five percent success. Sixty-five percent success. Our mantra. We didn't have sex for twenty-three days and felt buoyant, freed from conscription. On the twenty-third night, Noah brought home sushi, two bottles of rice wine, and kissed me long and hard, and for the first time in months, making love seemed like a natural way to spend an evening.

"Take these off," Noah said, smoothing his hands over my breasts to the elastic of my sweatpants, snapping the waistband against my stomach, pushing them down from my hips.

We made love on the floor. At first, Daisy sniffed around us, curious at this new abandon, then, realizing that we had simply shifted location, retreated, bored, to the couch.

Still, though, I couldn't concentrate, kept imagining all those millions of sperm flicking their tails, straining and heaving and dying, desperate to make it to that egg. I sighed, tried to roll out from under him.

"Don't." Noah pinned me down. "Look at me," he said.

I opened my eyes. "It's no use." His thighs clenched around me. My body fell flat against the floor.

"This isn't about making babies."

"I can't."

"Say, 'Fuck me, Noah.'" He pushed against me. "I can wait all night."

"Fuck you," I said.

He pushed again. "Good, talking dirty. That's a start. Say it again."

"Fuck you, Noah"

"Now you've got us fucking each other," he said into my ear.

"Yes," I said.

That night I slept with my hand stretched across my belly hoping against hope to feel the movement, the energy, the vibrations of cells multiplying and dividing, growing and growing.

For weeks, I willed myself to forget Lizzie, my anger, her soon-to-not-be-pregnancy, and threw myself into work, deciding to make the Ms. Buckner a beautiful bride. The day before the Buckner wedding, I was out of bed by three, slugging down scalding coffee and on the Expressway thirty minutes later. The flower mart in College Point opened at 4:30 and I wanted to be early. But that's how I liked it, the vendors pulling up their trucks and vans, hauling buckets of flowers; the petals closed in tight fists, ready to uncurl during the day.

Except for the terrible fluorescent light humming from street lamps, it was quiet. I bought coffee and an egg sandwich from the corner diner and sat on a bench that smelled of cat piss, watching vendors angle and arrange flowers in their stalls, shifting a bucket of calla lilies for sunflowers, peonies for dahlias.

That morning, I needed silver Shrimp flowers, French lilacs, and miniature pompoms that would be trimmed and shaped into "rough hewn" bouquets; I was not supposed to artfully arrange them in planned clusters, but was to toss them together as if I'd just collected them from a kitchen garden without deliberation or pretension to grandeur. Ms. Buckner, the bride, had called five times in the past three days: *No baby's breath. No garden ever has that. The bridesmaids are going for a Pre-Raphaelite look. So make the flowers nymphy, a little dangerous.*

Would a juicy Venus-flytrap suffice? I really had no idea what this woman wanted. No, that's not it. I knew what she wanted but I didn't know why she needed a florist, a fact I'd pointed out months before in the planning stage of her meticulously calculated, slipshod wedding.

"I don't have the time or inclination," she replied. "Think wildflower chic."

The bride-to-be was paying four hundred dollars for obscenely superfluous flowers that would be woven into the fringes of the goddess and attending nymphettes' five-hundred-dollar-a-piece, rough-hewn bouquets. I wasn't complaining.

Jerry, the vendor of the exotics, babied his buds. The Shrimp flowers, Parrot tulips, stars-of-Bethlehem, and Amazon lilies were encased in individual water vials inside a state-of-the-art flower fridge with built-in sprinklers that kept the blooms at an optimum temperature and accurately moist. The flowers all gathered and loaded into the back of my Suburban, Jerry warned, "You should get them to a refrigerator soon if you want to keep them fresh for tomorrow. They don't take to this climate too well, and they don't like the stuffy heat of a car."

It was early, and they could hold for a few hours, and since my assistant was opening the shop that morning, I decided to drive into the city to see JoJo.

My mother refused to step foot in JoJo's apartment, called it a hovel for crack addicts. JoJo, a junior at Parsons, lived in a sixth floor walk-up in the East Village. Before my parents agreed to let her move out of the dorms to a place of her own, Dad installed burglar bars on the two windows and insisted on paying for an alarm service. JoJo balked, said she wasn't looking for suburban safety, that her art needed to reflect the gritty aspects of Real Life, that her friends would laugh at her, which Mom countered by stating that she was studying Fine Art, not Performance Art. Dad said that he understood, but the alarm system would give them peace of mind; they could be sure that she wouldn't be the latest victim of some serial cannibalist who boiled little red-haired girls for dinner. But whenever Mom and Dad came up from Naples (they retired to Florida for golf, tennis, and luxury condominium living), they either met JoJo in restaurants like covert spies, or at my house, safe, neutral territory. Mom's standard issue line: "I've lived too long to have to start worrying about stepping on crack needles."

JoJo rolled her eyes. "It's heroin now, Mom. Not crack."

"You mean heroin *again*, JoJo," my mother replied.

I reached the apartment by six-thirty, too early for JoJo, but what else was I going to do? I knocked and knocked, and finally she opened the door, hair in two messy red pigtails, wrapped in a Mickey Mouse sheet, a pair of fuzzy pink kitty slippers on her feet, and nothing else. She looked like a depraved twelve-year old.

"You just let anyone in without asking who it is?" I handed over a bunch of sunflowers.

She sighed. "Don't give me shit. It's too early and I'm too hung over." She sniffed at the petals. "They don't smell."

"They're not supposed to," I said.

She padded into the kitchen, the long whiskers on the slippers brushing the floor, and returned, the flowers bobbling in a tall plastic cup, an inch of water barely covering the stems. She flopped across the couch and closed her eyes.

"God, I'm tired," she yawned.

"Don't you ever sleep?"

She shrugged. "Not at night," she said. "Not when the room's spinning."

I found a bottle of Advil in my purse, shook out three, and passed them to her.

"Always thinking," she said and gulped them down with a sip of sunflower water. "What the hell are you doing here this early?"

I lifted her head, sat down, rested her head back on my lap. "Out getting flowers, and decided to see you."

"Nobody goes for a drive at five in the morning. That's not natural. You need to get a life. Have kids or something instead of ruining a perfectly good hangover."

I tugged her mass of red hair out from under her neck and sifted it back and forth between my hands.

She snuggled closer. "God that feels good," she sighed. "Ian never does that. All he want to do is screw."

"Save the details."

"Look," she said, and opened her mouth wide. She waggled her tongue and its accompanying silver stud spiked clean through to the underside. "I got it a few nights ago. Not that I really remember getting it. Ian got his done too."

"Disgusting," I said. "Revolting. It looks like a meat hook. That's not natural."

"It's supposed to be great for blowjobs and vice versa."

"Shouldn't it be great already?"

"I don't know, big sister. You tell me."

What could I tell her since there hadn't been any in months, since the only sex I'd had was un-reproductive? So we sat in silence as I rolled her hair into two corkscrew spirals around her ears.

"You fucked up big time," she finally said.

"I know," I rested my hands on her head. Her hair unwound and spilled over her shoulders.

"Lizzie doesn't want to talk to you. I can't change her mind and I can't blame her."

"That's not why I came."

"Yes it is," she said and sat up. "There's something else I should tell you."

"She's having me excommunicated?"

"I went with her."

Steady, Annie, steady. I kissed the top of her head. "I have these ridiculous flowers suffocating in my trunk. I have to go."

JoJo draped an arm across my back, clutched my shoulder, trying to pull me to her for a hug.

If I let my body go soft, it would fall apart. "Those sunflowers will die without more water," I said. "But not too much, otherwise they'll rot."

By the time I got back home, the Shrimp flowers had wilted. I sprayed miniature tea roses silver and hoped Ms. Buckner wouldn't notice, at least until the bouquet had dried out in some long, forgotten box stuffed under a bed. She'd wonder at all that silver dust, but by then, it wouldn't matter to a long-standing wife, mother of two, or recent childless divorcée.

Even though it was late October, I transplanted all the mature, blooming tulips into the front garden, then cleaned out the greenhouse until all that was left were trails of soil on the low tables, and shriveled leaves kicked into corners.

Noah thought I was crazy. "You'll kill them. All that hard work."

"That's the point. Perfect rows of perfect tulips. It's time to see what they're made of. Either the bulbs make it to spring or they all die. Either way, I'm finished with them." I snapped off a bloom and handed it to him.

Noah chucked it over the fence into the neighbor's yard.

"I don't care," I said.

He broke off another blossom, threw it at me. It hit my chest then fell to the ground. "You don't care?" he said.

I shook my head, mashed the bloom with the heel of my shoe.

He walked off. I continued with the work.

Noah watched me from a lounge chair for the next two hours, waiting for god-knows-what. When I finished, he dragged the mower behind him across the lawn and paused at the end of the flower beds, nodded, then gunned the motor and pushed it slowly across the tulips. Red heads and green leaves blew out behind the whirring blades like confetti, though in celebration of nothing. When the bed was leveled, he cut the motor. The silence was strange, somehow deflating.

"You might as well be deliberate and get it over with so
we can get on with our lives."

For days after, I went out in the early mornings and sat
in the empty greenhouse, shivering without the heat lamps
and the heaters, the cold cutting right through the panes
of glass. There was nothing to do, nothing I wanted to do
except to fill up the space again with growing things. I
turned to wildflowers, perhaps an anomaly in a hothouse, but
they were more real than my tulips. Sturdier. Independent.
Imperfect with wills of their own. It came down to survival
of the fittest. Strong roots, little water, quick growth. No
need for heat lamps and hydrogenated water. They were
genetically predisposed to fend for themselves.

My choices were irrational—names that I liked, names
that were difficult to roll off the tongue, that made me
trip and stumble, and laugh at my ineptitude. *Matelea
gonocarpa, Gaillardia puichella, Heterotheca subauxillaris,
Commelina erecta, Ipomoea alba.* Fertile, fecund-sounding
blooms, commonly known as climbing milkweed,
firewheel, camphorweed, day flower, moonflower. Weeds
that sounded like the tests we went through that fall. First
the *Hysteroscopy:* a thin telescope, warmed inside a mini-
microwave, slid through my vagina, then cervix; its tiny,
mechanical eyeball peeping at the empty, inner cavity of my
uterus, checking for defects. Then the *Hysterosalpinogram:*
my uterus and fallopian tubes lit up on an x-ray by a white,
opaque dye; they looked like ghosts, hollow shells. Noah's
sperm did not escape unscathed, became participants in a
battery of timed races. In The *Hamster-Zona Free Ovum
Test,* his sperm hurdled over each other, each trying to be
the first to penetrate a hamster egg; then *Penetrak,* his sperm
clocked as they swam through cow mucus. I didn't really

understand the point of his tests in the end since his sperm would have to swim through me, penetrate my eggs, not Old MacDonald's.

Bottom-line: Noah's sperm were not at fault.

"Not that infertility is anyone's fault," Doctor Shinefeld announced at our fourth appointment, "but the sperm are not the problem."

Noah exhaled, perceptibly relieved.

I was disappointed. Not that I wanted to blame Noah. I just didn't want it to be me.

"Annie," the doctor continued, patting my back this time, "it's your eggs. LUH. *Luteinized Unruptured Follicle Syndrome.*"

Noah squeezed my hand in sympathy. I pulled it from him.

Doctor Shinefeld swiveled in half pivots, pushing off his left foot, then right, then left, then right, and twirled his mustache. "If you recall, LUH is a dysfunction in which ripe eggs aren't released from the follicle. So the fimbria, the little fingers that catch the egg and deliver it to the fallopian tube, come up empty-handed."

I laughed. "My follicle is dysfunctional? What? Like some empty grab bag?"

"Stop it," Noah whispered, and touched his finger to my hand, a light stroke across my knuckles. "I'm sorry," he said, "Annie's just upset."

"The good news is," Dr. Shinefeld said, oblivious to our interruptions, though the chair was still for once, "you are perfect candidates for in vitro."

I only told my mother, not wishing the topic of my imperfect womb to radiate out through the feeder roots to the different branches of the family.

My mother, understandably, had reservations, her disapproval loud and clear even over the phone wires. "Test tubes? Haven't you heard about all the couples who wind up having eight kids at once?"

"Not test tubes. Petri dishes, Mom." I shifted the receiver and flipped the page of the cookbook. "Do you know where I can get kalonji seeds?"

"What is that? Some kind of hallucinogen JoJo's talked you into?"

"They're for cooking. I'm making mango chutney." I added the seeds to my shopping list: fennel, ginger, mangoes.

"But what about all those drugs, Annie. Who knows what they'll do to your body. Or your child's, like all those poor DES babies with hands growing out from their shoulders." She clucked her tongue.

"It's not like that."

"Can't you keep trying? You're young. What about adoption? If it's the money, we could help you out. They have brokers now that can bump you up a list." She tapped the phone against something, the table maybe, as if trying to knock sense into me all the way from Florida.

"My eggs are being harvested in two weeks. A jumbo Grade A dozen."

"So it's as simple as harvesting and growing a bacteria culture for strep?" she demanded.

"Not everyone has the luxury to just do it and get pregnant."

Thus began a week of injections of Pergonal and Metrodin in the rear muscles of my left and right hips. It was difficult to aim straight-on since I had to crane my neck around to get a good look so I turned the job over to Noah.

He sat on the edge of the tub, held his breath and pulled a square of skin tight between two fingers, then guided the needle down into muscle, wincing every time. Only after he'd pulled out the needle, then drew permanent, red magic-marker circles on the fresh puncture to avoid the sore spots the next morning, did he breathe again.

"What a sorry pair of junkies we are," he laughed one night. "Are you sure this is legal and not just some homegrown Texas bullshit the doctor's been giving us?"

I scowled. "If you don't want to do this, don't. I can manage on my own."

He apologized and pressed his lips to the black-and-blue skin. "Don't ever say I didn't kiss your ass," he said.

Sleep was impossible. I was waiting to feel my ovaries kick into overproduction, for my eggs to line up into little rows, soldiers and soldierettes, marching off to battle. Maybe none of them would make it: twelve could-have-beens-but-never-would-bes. Or only one would make it. Natural selection: the hardiest egg survives, the remaining eleven, weak runts without a chance, die. I told Noah I couldn't sleep because I could feel the eggs moving into formation.

"Come on, Annie," he groaned, "the hormones are screwing with you. Just relax and don't think about it."

"I can't help it."

"You can."

But I couldn't help it. All I could do that week was poke and prod my abdomen, where I thought the follicles might be and imagine that they were stuffed with eggs, soft, ripe eggs, squashed into each other like fish roe.

Lizzie called back, almost two months after the fact. I was in the greenhouse, trimming back the Firewheels which were about to go to seed, trying to prolong the bloom cycle by a few weeks.

Her first words, not "Hello," or "I've missed you," or "I forgive you," but, "Annie, how could you?"

I readied myself for a long-overdue scolding.

Her voice tightened and I imagined the tops of her knuckles turning white. "Does JoJo know? I had to hear it from Mom." Her voice went soft, anger spilling out and away. "And don't play dumb."

I was silent.

"Mom told me that you can't have a baby."

"I can. I just need help." My hand rested on my belly, on top of the follicles again, searching for signs.

"A surrogate? Because if that's what you mean, I'll do it."

"Lizzie, your logic fails me. You won't have your own baby but you'd have mine?"

"I'm going to hell," she snuffled.

"So am I, so even-steven. Besides, I don't want your fetus. I want my own. Not Lizzie and Kevin's or Lizzie and Noah's. Annie and Noah's. So stop crying."

She blew her nose. "Have you seen JoJo's tongue? I almost puked."

I could have been put under for the egg retrieval, but I wanted to be awake and aware, wanted to know they were there. I opted for localized anesthesia, felt the probe move up through my vagina, but then felt nothing, not even the tickle or twinge of feeling as the needle slid through the ovaries and suctioned the eggs. Nothing to let me know it was happening at all. I smiled anyway, sleepy and dazed, imagining the eggs swimming up through the needle, then burrowing, feet first, into flats filled with soil. Tiny green shoots pushing up and out, then the blooming heads of babies.

"There. All done," Doctor Shinefeld said. The green mask covered his face, so all I could see was the imprint of his mustache against the cloth, and his eyes, looming big and round behind goggles, saucers with eyebrows. He was a giant green bee, and as he pulled out the needle and the probe, I felt my insides curl up, petals closing in on themselves.

I giggled. "You got all of them? Every last one? There could be more in hiding."

And then it was Noah, blurry, bleary, sipping a Coke, and cramps that flashed hot and cold across my abdomen, down my thighs.

He smoothed my hair back, held a cold washcloth to my forehead, and said, "Success. Nine eggs are being fertilized as we speak. My sperm couldn't wait to get a crack at them. It is strange, though. We're producing without reproducing. I mean I know it works and we'll still be parents, not simply donor hosts, but somehow it feels unnatural, not quite legitimate."

"Shut up," I said, and then threw up all over myself. Yellow mucus, mine, not a cow's.

Doctor Shinefeld called it *assisted hatching:* four eggs fertilized, three transferred back to my uterus for implantation.

The following week, I was a nervous wreck. My assistant had to fill most of the orders; I tried a few, but my balance was off—I couldn't pair complimentary colors, couldn't arrange filler flowers so bouquets didn't look cheap, couldn't trim roses without stabbing my thumb on a thorn or snapping their heads off. I couldn't keep my hands off my belly, trying to feel if all three were developing or if all three were dead, convinced that like some faith healer, the rough pads of my fingertips could divine miracles, conduct God, could affect the very chemistry, biology, fecundity of my cells.

But when I kept Noah up one night until 2 A.M., demanding that he, too, feel what I most certainly must be feeling, the rumblings of our cells coming together, he said, "Annie, you can't feel cellular movement. It's just gas."

The next morning, three flats of flowers, packed in giant moving crates, arrived at my door with a note attached: *Discovered by a horticultural scientist while vacationing in North Florida. Take care of them. The shipping cost a fortune. Love, Mom.*

It had been a long time since anyone sent flowers, even Noah. He stopped after our first anniversary, complaining that I would find fault with the florist, that I would know the cost, call him cheap, none of which ever crossed my mind, but I supposed I would find fault, be able to garner the cost right down to the tax. So he presented theater tickets, movie tickets, concert tickets, anything that wasn't expected or known, anything to get me out of the greenhouse. But Mom knew better, knew that I needed something with leaves and roots and stems and petals, something that would grow.

So she sent *Hymenocallis godfreyi*, Spider lilies. I carefully pinned the mother leaves to damp sand, spreading them back so as not to damage the pale yellow, trumpet-shaped flowers. With a sharp, curved knife, I sliced off the baby shoots that rooted from the ribs, pinched them carefully between miniature forceps, then buried the seedlings in empty pots of soil. The lilies were sprayed down until water pooled in the center of the leaves. Four hours passed, four blissful hours when I did not rub my belly, did not worry about my body failing, did not wish for anything but the mere survival of what was already before me.

Later that afternoon, Noah and I grilled steaks, kicked a tennis ball around with Daisy, then stretched out, side-by-side in lounge chairs buried under wool blankets.

"They called," he said, without looking at me. I felt light-headed and knew.

"When?"

"Yesterday morning." He jumped up and kicked the tennis ball across the lawn. Daisy loped after it, skidded in the grass, then bounded back, dropping the ball at Noah's feet. He kicked it across the lawn and she took off after it again. She nosed for the ball in a shrub, pawing at the branches, then ran back, successful, again. He patted Daisy's head. "One more time, girl." He kicked the ball and sent it ricocheting against a tree. Daisy trotted after it, flopped down, and gnawed on the ball.

Instinct. It should be that easy.

"So I'm the last to know." That would explain my mother's extravagance.

"They said we can try again with the next cycle."

"No," I said. "No. Not yet. Not for a while."

He held my hand and we sat together until mosquitoes and fireflies crept out of the grass, and Daisy whimpered and nudged our legs with her cold nose, hungry for dinner.

I worked, without direction, with the Spider lilies. They grew into wild, extended clusters, their petals, blooms, and stalks intermingled, wrapping around each other's stakes in knots of red and green. One night, a storm came up out of nowhere; the sky cracked into fault lines. Work was impossible, so I stretched out on the floor, on top of discarded cuttings, scattered petals, and clumps of dirt, and stared up through the glass roof at the sky, empty now of stars.

In the silent moment between the flash of light and the distant boom of sound, I saw her, then felt her inside of me. She was Noah and she was me. The curve of her nose was Noah, the arch of her brow me. Our child, growing inside my belly, pushing against my sturdy ribs, swelling inside my broken heart. Then it thundered and she was gone, fragmenting back into the scattered particles of unrealized cells.

I lay there for a long while, willing her back. But nothing happened, just more lightning, more thunder, more empty space. Noah found me on the floor.

"Annie, wake up."

But I was awake.

"What happened?"

"Nothing." I said. "I was tired and now you're here."

I reached for Noah, for his body, solid and sure and natural beside mine.

VIGIL

Normally, before the divorce, my mother would have been going to the beach with us, dressed in her black bathing suit with the built-in tummy sucker, floppy straw hat with the chewed brim, and flip-flops which protected her feet from discarded syringes. Normally she would have proclaimed this to be a perfect beach day—slight breeze, a few clouds to take the edge off the sun, a new Danielle Steele book to read. But she was no longer normal. She was on her way to colon therapy. Once a month, Dr. Grabo, her holistic healer, cleaned her colon of the dietary toxins and his assistant massaged her temples with aromatic oils. My mother assured us it was a comfortable cleansing; not the run-of-the-mill enema.

My mother rummaged under the seat, pulling out used tissues, yoga fliers, fuzzy lifesavers, flattened raisins, and a tube of SPF 30 which she pressed into Kara's hand. "Just use it for once," she begged, "otherwise you'll look like Grandma Joe." This was my mother's threat every summer. Grandma Joe's skin was cross-stitched with wrinkles.

Kara had been working on the ideal tan since the first sunny days of March. She sat in the backyard surrounded by tinfoil reflectors, face turned up to the sun, shivering in her bikini, as the last of the snow melted. By July, she had reached maximum color, a deep even bronze.

"Or you'll get skin cancer," my mother continued. "Lesions, on the side of your nose. Great, big, cavernous lesions."

Kara's nose was smooth and freckle-free, her vanity unfazed by the dire predictions. "There'll be a cream or pill by then," she said, handing the tube back to my mother.

Since the divorce, my mother had become convinced that our newfound happiness and security was threatened by a toxic world; and Kara, convinced that the future promised an all-purpose Super Cream that would cure every ill: wrinkles, skin cancer, pimples, and PMS.

My mother passed the sunblock. "Here Gina, you still have baby skin." Kara laughed, I stuck my tongue out. My mother apologized for the unintended insult. "All I meant is that there's still hope for you."

Now thirteen, I no longer had baby skin, had indeed been the first of my friends to go to the dermatologist to get my very own prescription cream. Allison and Jeannie were jealous of my jump start on clear skin. Sometimes I brought the tube to school to share, and they talked wistfully of the day when their mothers would spring for a professional consultation.

My mother reset the radio back to her AM talk show and sighed, "Can the two of you try to get along for the afternoon? Kara, remember I'm trusting you to watch out for Gina. And don't swim if there's an undertow." And then she kissed us off, leaving us alone.

We walked to the edge of the boardwalk and Kara stopped, rolled the waist of her cutoffs past her hipbones, pulled off her tee-shirt, adjusted the straps of her bikini and said, "Just don't sit near me, okay?"

"Are you meeting Sean?" Kara kept her diary in the closet with my father's things, the things left behind: *Star Wars* video collection, one scuffed wing-tip shoe, dirty sock stuffed inside, suit forgotten at the dry cleaners, four rolls of undeveloped film from the last family vacation on Cape Cod, his box of business cards: *Vincent DiFerrari, Assistant Regional Manager, Westec Residential Alarm Systems*, and a shoebox full of shot glasses pocketed from bars across Long Island's South Shore. It was the only place in the house my mother consciously avoided. We referred to it as *that* closet. The chafing dish was in *that* closet, could I get it? The big golf umbrella was in *that* closet, top shelf, could Kara reach it? *That* closet became Kara's own private confessional. In her diary, hidden behind a box of old slides, Kara wrote that she had almost gone all the way with Sean. They were at a keg party and snuck off into a bedroom, and she let him feel her up and down but he wasn't mature enough to be The One.

Kara swung her beach bag over her shoulder and stepped out into the sand. "Fifteen feet, Gina. That's as close as you come."

My mother read *Psychology Today,* snipping articles and tacking them to the refrigerator with post-it notes on top. Kara—Read This!! Gina—This One's For You!! She left articles about depression next to my cereal bowl in the morning, about body image under Kara's Fat Free yogurt container, about mother-daughter dynamics taped to the bathroom mirror. Citing her experts, she explained that Kara was asserting her boundaries since she was sixteen going on seventeen, since we shared a room, since I was the younger sister, since she was becoming an *individuated* woman, whatever that meant. Basically, following the experts' advice, she devised a system. Kara and I each had the bedroom to ourselves for one uninterrupted hour each day. I didn't use my hour, but I knew how Kara used hers; I could hear her chanting, "I love my breasts and they love me. Soon they'll grow to a 36C." She had actually reached the low end of a B-cup, an accomplishment worth noting at family dinners. Aunt Susie, Aunt Patty, and Grandma Joe said that it must have been the Italian blood from our father's side, and then they sized up my chest and said maybe it was just a fluke.

Besides creative visualization, Kara also practiced kissing on the wall, covering it with closed-mouth smooches, pursed-puckers, and open-O's in plums and reds and pinks, the range of Revlon colors. My mother said that when this stage passed we'd just paint over it in a color of my choice. I knew if our father still lived with us the wall would have remained the original Rose Petal Pink.

But after the divorce, my mother had grown understanding of Kara's emotional turbulence. For two months, Kara stopped talking, cut school, ran away to friends' houses. She finally opened her mouth about two weeks before Christmas and asked to be taken to the Gap to pick out her presents. My mother returned the clothes she'd picked out at Macy's, afraid that her choices had been foolish—wrong sizes, wrong colors, wrong styles, not what Kara would want. Silence became Kara's means to a new wardrobe, new CD's, later curfews, locked bedrooms. At night, though, I heard her crying, face stuffed into the pillow, and when I crept into bed with her, she sometimes said she was okay, and rubbed my back, and we fell asleep next to each other. Usually she told me to leave her alone and stay out of her life.

Field 3, Jones Beach was known to all Long Islanders
as the singles bar of beaches. Muscle guys strutted around
in skimpy briefs, their penises swaying in the breeze like
external tonsils, their shoulders shined and buffed with
baby oil. They wore Gold's Gym tank tops and called girls
"babe." Groups of girls stretched across king-sized sheets,
stomachs pulled tight, backs arched, knees bent, poised like
Rockettes ready to do a kickline; they passed around the
Cosmo Quiz, "Heartbreaker or a Heartacher?," and misted
each other's bodies with Hawaiian Tropic Darque Tanning
Oil. And as long as people weren't drowning or puking in
the water, lifeguards ignored the beer.

Field 4 was the family beach: noses smeared white with
zinc oxide; fluorescent flowered beach umbrellas lined the
shore; skirted bathing suits covered saddlebags and cellulite;
bald spots concealed from the sun under an assortment of
caps, visors, and toupees; garbage cans filled with sand-
soggy diapers. There was mini-golf, bocci, volleyball, and
Italian ices.

I liked Field 4 because there were things to do; Kara
liked Field 3 because there were people to see.

Kara picked a patch of sand near a bunch of guys
building a beer wall with empty cans; it started at their
heads and traveled around the outer edge of the towels.
They were all wearing bathing suits of various plaids and
baseball caps with names of colleges. Kara flapped her
blanket in the breeze and let it settle. She shimmied out
of her cutoffs, dripped baby oil down her legs, over her
stomach, up her arms, and trailed lip balm over her mouth
with her fingertips. I watched the guys nudge each other
and watch her. But Kara just stretched and sighed and
went to sleep. I counted off fifteen feet and set up camp

a little less melodramatically: bath towel, SPF 30, salami sandwich, thermos of Tang, mystery book. I didn't want to be noticed, didn't want their strange eyes wandering over my skinny, level body.

My father kept a stash of *Playboys* in the attic, not hidden in some dark corner, but in stacks next to the Christmas Tree box. I don't know why he saved them all, all the pictures looked the same. Naked women wrapped in gauze or posed in front of rain smudged windows or sprawled on animal skin rugs. They didn't look remotely like me, or how I even thought I might look. They were big, and full, and unashamed. The only part of the magazine that I could relate to was the personal data page for the centerfolds: they liked tennis, poetry, bagels, kindness; they disliked boxing, dishonesty, pot roast, golf. I didn't like to think of my father looking at all those naked women, all those bodies.

An hour passed quietly; I read, Kara slept, the guys drank and stayed carefully to themselves. When Kara woke, she flipped to her stomach, ran her fingers under the bikini bottoms, adjusting the elastic, unzipped her backpack, and unwrapped a can from a layer of tinfoil. She cracked the beer open, sipped, and smiled at the guys.

I knew Kara drank; she hid a bottle of vodka behind a pile of stuffed animals crammed under her bed. Paddington Bear, Cabbage Patch Kid, and Garfield were her partners in crime. Before she went out with her friends, she drank vodka from an "Italian Stallion" shot glass left over from Dad Days. She hid that in a drawer behind her hidden Victoria's Secret underwear. She knew I knew, said drinking wasn't such a big deal, that Dad just didn't know how to drink. Late at night I heard her in the bathroom throwing up, gagging, flushing, and brushing her teeth. My mother hadn't noticed, which was strange because she could smell a gas leak five blocks over, or my dad's whiskey breath through

a sinus infection. I could smell it on Kara. She smelled like
my dad only sweeter. Mom only smelled her patchouli.

My mother was on a "healing journey"; she'd been
going to a therapy group called "Visualizing the New You—
Learning to Break with the Stale Self." (Hence Kara's boob
mantra.) She started burning patchouli instead of Garden
Fresh potpourri, wore silver earrings instead of pearl knots,
and nodded with understanding when I said I failed my
history test. Over cups of herbal tea, she comforted, "Sister
Thomas just doesn't know how to teach the French and
Indian War with imagination."

During the divorce, Mom made piles and piles of grilled
cheeses. French Toast, grilled with cheese, for breakfast,
grilled cheese with tomatoes for lunch, grilled cheese with
bacon for dinner. She bought Velveeta by the crate and
stored loaves of bread in the freezer just in case she ran out.
After the first few weeks of this feeding frenzy, I suggested
we go to the diner for salads, burgers, anything non-cheesy,
to which she replied, "That's okay. I love grilled cheese," with
the same gusto she used when announcing, "That's okay. I
love the gristly pieces." She ate grilled cheese because that's
all that was left for her, all that she was hungry for. For my
father, she cooked full-palate meals: steak with peppercorn
sauce, herbed potatoes, green beans almondine, and black
forest cake. For herself, she could only cook bland food;
she said her taste buds had shriveled up the day my father
moved out. In five months, Mom gained forty pounds,
popped the buttons on skirts, gave up on zippers, and only
wore pants with elastic waistbands.

The day she signed the divorce papers, she stood in
front of the full-length mirror in her underwear and cried,
pinching the folds of her stomach, the skin under her arms,
the bottom of her butt. And then suddenly she stopped and

glared back at herself. "Never again," she said to us, "will
you see me like this." She rummaged through her sewing
box, handed Kara a tape measure, handed me a pencil and
paper, and demanded the measurements of her waist, hips,
thighs, calves, neck, chest, even her ankles. "Nothing," she
said, "will go unaccounted for."

I watched from the bed, catching Kara's puzzled and
fearful glances in the mirror as she circled my mother's
body like a tailor, wrapping the tape around one thigh, then
the other, calling out numbers that lost their meaning as I
wrote them in little columns: chest-41, thigh-19, ankle- 8,
rear end-53. From that day on, Kara and I had to measure
my mother weekly, adding, subtracting, pulling the tape
tighter to make the numbers smaller. Little by little, she
shrank, her body began to disappear, until I knew we had
lost her.

While on her "journey," she gave up caffeine, sugar, and
fat; instead, she drank herbal teas, got her colon cleaned, had
a friend named Helen, an expert in the "re-birthing" process.
Helen wanted to guide me through my "rebirth"; she said it
would help me "keep a whole self while going through the
fragmenting experience of adolescence." I declined; from
what I saw of the birth movie in religion class, it was bad
enough the first time. Helen and Mom went to Weight
Watchers, joined a ladies-only gym, meditated to fake birds'
songs in the living room.

Kara and I were left to ourselves. I was partial to
luncheon meat—salami, bologna, ham, anything but olive
loaf; Kara picked at salads, claimed she was getting fat, that
she inherited Mom's body and had to start "regulating" her
food. She even counted the calories in toothpaste.

Kara threatened death if I ratted on her drinking, which
I didn't believe, but wouldn't test. We shared a bedroom so

it would have been easy for her to smother me with a pillow in the middle of the night or cut out my tongue with her nail scissors. I wouldn't have said anything though.

My mother told Helen over the phone that she was still "grieving" over the divorce, and maybe she just needed a week away from it all—Kara, me, Massapequa, Long Island—to kick back on a Caribbean Island, swinging in a hammock, drinking root juices out of coconut shells. Helen offered to babysit, said my mother should rediscover her needs while she was still young, "Hell, have a fling with a sailing instructor in Aruba." But Mom said she was out of vacation time, even out of personal days, and besides, didn't feel like a fling with a twenty-year old who would want to have sex with the lights on.

I didn't want to upset my mother's grieving process with the news that Kara was drinking like our father. I didn't want Helen to "rebirth" me while babysitting. I didn't want to think of my mother having a fling.

There isn't much to do at the beach by yourself except to look at people between catnaps, or stare at the sand. I watched the way girls walked at the water's edge in pairs, how they passed men, swishing their feet slowly through the surf or walking heel-toe through the sand, defiant and proud, or slouching, arms crossed over stomachs. I watched couples grease each other, make-out, give wedgies, unhook straps. I watched the gulls steal bits of pretzels, bread, garbage. I found ten cigarette butts, six beer caps, two tampons, and one condom, smashed, buried, and forgotten in the sand. An old man wandered up from Field 4, skimming the sand with a metal detector. He'd stop, dig furiously with a small spade, pick something out and toss it away.

Once, my father rented a metal detector. Kara and I spent hours pacing the beach with him in the late afternoon, which was, according to him, "the best time for loot." The people would be gone, and all the lost money, broken necklaces, forgotten watches would be ours for the picking. He said we could keep anything we found as long as it wasn't historical, since, after all, pirates had buried treasure in these shifting sands. He told us about doubloons worth millions, about chests filled with jewels, about all we could do with the money. Kara found three dollars worth of change; I found a gold chain, twisted and tarnished, the clasp missing. My father looked at it, held it up to the fading sun, and tossed it back out to the sea. It was junk, he said, "electroplated crap." He returned the detector, said it was a waste of money and vacation time. Kara whispered to me that he was wrong, that I had found gold and he just didn't know it.

After the old man had disappeared down the beach, I watched Kara, how she played with the ends of her hair, twisting it around her fingers, how she let her bikini straps slide down her shoulders, how she wiggled her toes and swatted at imaginary sandflies. By the end of the second hour, they were all friends, the six plaid guys and Kara. They talked about school, college, and Kara lied, said she was a sophomore at Penn State, one of the names not written in hunter green across their caps. I watched her drink three beers of her own and stack them neatly by her side. By the end of the third hour, she drank two beers from their cooler. They adjusted the beer wall so her blanket fit inside. She talked mostly to a guy called Murphy, junior, University of Michigan, PoliSci major, burned shoulders. He sat closest to her, passing beers, bumping into her side. He offered to re-oil her, and Kara smiled, leaned into her knees, offered her back. His hands moved confidently over her shoulders, under her straps, and she giggled. My sister was ticklish along her sides. She didn't kick him away like she would have kicked me.

My sister called me a snoop, a busybody, a brat. My mother told me to give Kara breathing room. But there was no one else to smell breath and count meals. No one else to pay attention.

My mother worried that I was too detached from my father, that I took so completely to the divorce, was happy he was gone. She said it wasn't natural, that I was blocking, repressing, denying, that one day she'd be watching television, and there I would be, center stage, head resting on some talk show host's shoulder, telling all the world that the reason I killed was because of my parents' divorce. I wasn't sullen or hostile like Kara, so she was convinced that my easy adjustment was a honeymoon period, that in the years to come, I would have relationship problems, hate men, have boyfriends who gave me black eyes.

I don't know why she couldn't understand that I was happy he left. Happy that she stopped eating grilled cheeses, stopped crying, stopped nursing hangovers, calming anger, closing doors. Happy that I couldn't react like Kara. I could only watch her, stick close, play her shadow. Because who else would have known where she hid her vodka, her diary, her ticklish spots?

Murphy anchored his feet in the sand and tugged Kara up from her towel. She swayed back and forth, as if the weight of the breeze could knock her around like a styrofoam cup. He draped his arm around her shoulder and they stumbled around towels, radios, legs, and coolers to the water. I followed, keeping my distance. When they were thigh deep, Murphy lunged and tackled her; Kara screeched, landing hard in shallow water. I laughed. She looked so stupid smiling up at Murphy, as if it didn't hurt at all. Murphy shrugged and paddled out deeper.

I swam after them, parallel to them, bobbed up for air, trying to catch their words, but could only hear them laughing between the waves. And then they were kissing. Kara had her legs wrapped around his back; Murphy had his fingers under her straps, tried to unhook the back of her bikini. Kara slapped at his chest and screeched again. I dove under the water and swam back to shore.

I was good at keeping track of things. At school, I could always tell who had a new haircut, a new boyfriend, a new jacket, who had their period, who didn't. I liked to know where people were. I liked to be the one with the information. I gave up on keeping track of my father. He went too far, always moving around, first Phoenix, then Las Vegas, Boca Raton, then Seattle; he had to keep up with the action, the next housing boom. He said there was a fortune to be made in the alarm business out West: new residents, new city, new fears. New York was dried up, the niche already filled. I didn't think his alarm prospects could be any better than New York, and so I suspected he didn't want to be kept track of, measured against the rest of us. I remember him drinking, remember his strangeness, how his words didn't sound right, how his movements seemed wrong. My mother used to call it "Daddy's make-believe time." She said, "Make believe Daddy's a lion. Remember at the zoo how loud they were?" Or, "Make believe it's just thunder and lightning. Just electricity and rain outside." When I was older, I counted his drinks and he yelled at me, said he didn't need anyone keeping track of him.

Kara doesn't remember, doesn't want to. All she remembers is the end. Mom smashing the empty bottles in the street. Mom packing Dad's clothes in boxes. Mom erasing the messages that asked for another chance.

Sometimes I felt that I was the only sane one left in our house, that I was the gauge measuring how far we'd wandered from each other. My mother had turned into a fuzzy smear of pastel colors and wheat germ. Kara had threatened my life. I was lonely, addicted to salami and afternoon talk shows that discussed dysfunction and co-dependence.

On their way back from the water, Murphy staggered over to the guys, rolled into the sand, and opened a beer. Kara detoured, stopped at my towel.

"Move it," I said. She was dripping water all over my book and blocking the sun.

"You're okay, right?" She plopped down and squeezed water from her hair.

"I'm fine."

She pulled her fingers through her hair, catching them in knots. "I'm covered in sand from head to toe," she said, and picked off the stray strands of hair that clung to her nails. "Aren't they cute, Gina? What about the guy I was with? Did you see us?"

"They seem older."

"That's the point. They are." She waved at them, but they were intent on a game of hackysack. Murphy tried to kick the hackysack and wiped out in the sand.

Kara pressed a finger into her belly and a white print appeared. "Look, Gina. I'm burning."

"Maybe we should call Mom."

Kara stood up. "I don't feel like leaving. And remember? Colon cleaning day."

"Then put on my 30. You should be more careful."

She traced the outline of white-skinned straps over her

shoulder. "Oh well. What's done is done. Four months of work wasted. Now I'll start to peel. You'll be here right? Because I'm going with Murphy. We're going to listen to the radio in his car. You'll watch my stuff?"

"But it's so hot."

"Please, Gina. I'll be back soon."

I sighed and nodded. Kara tiptoed up to Murphy and whispered in his ear. They walked back up the beach, to the boardwalk, and out into the parking lot. I watched their heads, mostly Kara's blond one, disappear down a row of cars.

I waited for them to return, squinted at every couple, every blond girl in a bikini, in a one-piece, in shorts. It didn't matter. I stood watch as the guys drank beer, drifted off to sleep. Every now and then, one would roll over and say something about Kara and Murphy, but mostly about Kara, and they would laugh. I hated them.

I thought about finding a lifeguard, explaining that I couldn't find my sister and she had my heart medication and I think she went out to the parking lot for sunscreen, but oh god, my heart was going crazy. I thought about pressing my face to every car window until I found them. I thought about throwing my sandwich at the plaid guys, waiting for the seagulls to attack, then demanding her release. Instead, I stood in the hot sand, without flip-flops, letting it burn my feet, hoping that the moment I couldn't stand the pain would be the moment they came back. I tried this ten times. I tried telepathy. I tried holding my breath. I tried to stare at the sun, tried to do the un-do-able and bring Kara back from what she was doing. I prayed.

I felt her shadow fall across my body before I saw her: it was light, then dark, and then it waited. I looked up.

Kara's hair was clumped in tangles from the salt, mascara smudged beneath her eyes, bikini top uneven. A mermaid gone bad.

"Are you okay?"

She shrugged and sat down. "Do I look a mess?"

A bruise sat on the curve of her neck, speckled red like a tetanus shot. I touched it and asked, "He hurt you?"

"A hickey. Oh my god, I've never had a hickey. It's gross and all, but kind of cool, right? Like a love tattoo."

"It looks like he bit you."

"He was a great kisser. And he's twenty. Can you believe that?"

The side of her bikini bottom was twisted around, the tag on the outside. I tried to tuck the tag in, untwist the material, but realized she'd have to take the bottoms off to straighten it out.

Kara's eyes were closed and she rocked back and forth. "Gina, I don't feel so good. Maybe I should go to the bathroom." She took a deep breath, said "Oh no," and I knew she was going to be sick. She threw up all over my towel and book, splattering my legs. She stopped herself quickly and sat straight, as if nothing had happened. "They didn't see that, did they?"

"Who?" I wiped my legs, dabbed the book with a clean corner of the towel, tried not to breathe in her fumes.

"Murphy. The guys. It didn't look like I was throwing up, right? I mean, it's not like I made a scene."

"What are you talking about? You just puked your guts in the middle of a crowded beach, all over yourself, all over me, and all you care about is how you looked puking?"

Kara began to cry.

I wiped a string of spit from her mouth with my sweatshirt. She looked terrible and smelled worse. "You look fine," I lied. "Besides, they weren't looking over here."

And that was the truth. They were all down at the water, throwing around a football. Murphy never looked back.

We stayed in the ladies room stall for an hour. Kara knelt in muddy water on concrete, and threw up again and again. I held her hair back, flushed the toilet, wiped the seat. All the way through the heaving though, she kept talking about him. "He's cute, isn't he? I gave him my number." Or, "Do I look any different? Any older? What'll I tell Mom when he calls?"

"Don't tell her anything," I answered, "and fix your bottoms. They're all twisted."

She didn't look any different, at least not in the way she wanted. Just messy and sad. Sister Mary Louis told us in Family Life Class that the day a girl loses her virginity out of wedlock is the saddest day of her life. I thought she was lying, trying to scare us, but maybe she knew how it turns out.

Kara fingered the tag. "That's funny. I didn't even notice I put them on wrong." She stepped out of them, right there, in front of me. Kara who locked the bedroom to change, who accused me of trying to sneak peeks, stepped out of her bottoms and untwisted them. But she couldn't pull them back on; her hands were shaking and she started crying again.

So I knelt in the puddle, placed her feet through the holes, tugged the bottoms up, past her knees, over her thighs, to her hips. And I peeked, quickly, not knowing what to look for. Except maybe blood.

During one of her pauses, I called home, left a message for my mother to pick us up ASAP, as soon as her colon was clean enough, because Kara was sick. I wanted to tell her that I hated her and Kara and my father and the stupid beach and guys but I didn't.

I left Kara sitting on the curb, sipping a Coke; her knees were scoured red, her hair pulled back up in a ponytail. I went back to the beach to gather our things, threw the towel, book, and Kara's empty cans in the garbage. The guys were flopped on their backs, sleeping, some snoring, the beer wall now a complete circle around the edges of their towels. Murphy was on the end, baseball cap covering his face, stomach bright pink. His arm was smeared with blue ink that had washed off. I wondered if he had memorized Kara's number. If he remembered she went to Penn State. That he bit the side of her neck.

We waited by the curb for a long time. It began to rain and the beach cleared out; lightning crackled across the water and there was a mad rush for cars. Everyone whined about the traffic, about the day being ruined, about wet bathing suits. Kara and I just sat there, shivering. I could tell she was searching the crowd, scanning the cars that pulled out of the lot. But she never tried to wave anyone down.

When my mother finally swung up, honking the horn and flashing headlights as if we could have missed her, as if we weren't the last ones left, Kara said, "Don't say anything to Mom about today, okay?" I nodded and Kara climbed into the backseat, I climbed into the front.

"I think there's some blankets in the back. I must have just caught the rain," Mom said. She didn't look at us and I wondered if she knew how late she was. I wondered where she had been.

Kara passed a blanket and I wrapped myself inside. We were quiet all the way to the parkway, listening to the garden hotline talk about mulching and pruning and beetles chewing through tomato plants. Mom stole glances at both of us while switching lanes. "Is something wrong?" she finally asked, turning down the radio. "I'm sorry I was late. But Dr. Grabo was behind schedule. A woman with colitis had an emergency. I came when I could."

"Kara doesn't feel well. She's sick," I said.

She twisted around. Kara was stretched across the seat. "Kara, honey, you feel sick?" She felt her forehead. "You feel okay. But god, look at you. I told you to be careful with the sun."

"I'm fine," Kara said "it's not that bad."

"She didn't wear the sunblock," I said.

"Your eyelids are practically purple. And your chest. You'll be covered in blisters, you know." Mom sighed. "I'll run a cold chamomile bath for you when we get home."

"I said I'm fine. So I'm fine. Just take it easy with the brakes and my stomach will be fine."

"You feel sick to your stomach? You just may have sunstroke. Do you know you can die from sunstroke? Gina, you didn't notice her burning up?"

I shrugged. "You can't see a sunburn right away. It comes out later."

For the rest of the ride we listened to the windshield wipers thump back and forth at top speed, keeping time, counting miles. My mother hummed along to her Rainforest Medley CD, a little off-key, hands clenched around the steering wheel; Kara breathed steadily in and out, sleeping I supposed; I counted off exits, waiting patiently for ours. It took an hour and a half because of the rain and lightning and an accident on the parkway. When we finally turned into the driveway and rolled to a stop, I had the courage to look back at Kara. Only she wasn't sleeping, she was curled up in the seat, eyes scrunched closed. And she was crying, but trying hard not to.

"Mom, would you look. I told you she was sick."

My mother saw her, maybe even smelled her, and nodded.

Kara threw up once more, and my mother held her hair back, pressed a washcloth to her forehead. Kara was furious, "Stop babying me, goddammit. I can take care of myself." Mom ignored her and ran the bath. She tried to help Kara out of her wet clothes, but Kara pushed her away.

My mother sighed and said, "Gina, why don't you give us some privacy. You can start dinner if you want. And close the windows so the rain doesn't get in." She hugged me to her, still smelling of patchouli but more like my mother. "She'll be fine, Gina. Just a ruined tan. Maybe she learned her lesson."

Kara stood in the middle of the bathroom, hair scraggly, body shaking, bikini straps hanging off her shoulders, arms folded tightly across her chest, and she said, so quietly I almost didn't hear, "Fuck you, Mom. You don't know anything."

My mother was silent, then shrugged. "Don't think I'm impressed, Kara. I've heard it all. But I'll forgive you for it. We'll chalk it up to hormones and sunburn, okay?" My mother tentatively smiled, but Kara didn't, she just glared back, with the same look my mother had in her eyes that day in front of the mirror, wild beyond anger, propelled by the determination to leave us all behind. I knew, at that moment, that I could never bring Kara back.

The lights went out at dusk. The electric company said a main power line went down and it would be a few hours, maybe morning, before it would be back on. I made salami sandwiches, dandelion-root iced tea, and lit candles. We sat around the table, not saying much, watching the storm through the sliding glass doors. A big limb from the oak tree snapped off, the patio table and umbrella blew over, the metal garbage can clattered down the driveway.

But inside the kitchen, we just sat, sipped tea and nibbled on the sandwiches, willing ourselves to forget what had happened. Kara massaged aloe vera lotion into her skin so she wouldn't peel and look like a leper. My mother talked about the healing properties of herbs, how dandelion root helped upset stomachs, depression, headaches, and irritability, a cure for all our ills that day. I let Kara French-braid my hair, sat still for her and didn't scream when she accidentally yanked too hard. Honestly, she could have pulled all my hair out and it wouldn't have mattered because it was like it used to be. When we were emptying the dishwasher, Kara whispered, "Thanks, Gina."

I bent over, to rescue a knife fallen way in back, and said, "You were careful, weren't you?"

She tugged on the end of my braid and tried to smile. "No problemo, Gina. We can pretend like today never happened."

Later, I left Kara and Mom together in the kitchen. I sat on the stairs hoping to hear confessions and apologies, reconciliation. I wanted something, I suppose, to make it all right again, something to absolve me, to relieve me from my watch.

 hen phones ring in the middle of the night, it can only mean one of two things: an accident with high school kids, crushed beer cans under back seats, a corner oak tree, tall silver lamppost; or, a death of a parent, expected from cancer, unexpected from heart attack, maybe stroke, only once from suicide. The telephone finally rang at our house, the second-to-last on the Brook Hollow Junior High phone chain, at 4:33 A.M.

My father and I picked up our phones just as the second ring tapered off, and at once, I knew it was more than an accident or death because it was Mr. Sullivan who said, "Jim?" Not Mrs. Sullivan. I held my breath, waiting for my father to clear his throat, before twisting the phone into position and settling greedily into the darkness, the bloodsucker of suffering, desperate, without conscience.

We both had phones on our bedside tables, and as a result, reached automatically across the dark and answered late night calls in tandem, always expecting that other voice, her voice. He said hello, I said nothing, just turned the talking end toward the ceiling so my breathing couldn't be heard and listened to conversations I wasn't supposed to nor ever meant to hear. When Timmy O'Brien and his girlfriend Maria Frizotti wrecked his parents' new BMW, the police found an ashtray filled with used condoms and an emptied twelve-pack of beer at their feet; when Anthony Ritchie flipped his moped, broke both legs and lost an eye, his blood was racing with cocaine; when Mrs. Simmons died from a slip in the tub, Mr. Simmons wouldn't let the police or medics into the house until after he had bathed his wife, dressed her in a favorite seersucker suit, lipsticked her mouth, and powdered her face.

I was interested in death in the way that my friends were interested in sex. They surreptitiously studied the mundane *Joy of Sex,* the exotic *Kama Sutra*, the horrible medical textbooks detailing genital diseases at the super bookstore in the mall. While theirs was a shared obsession, giggled over, attempted, mine remained secret, dependent upon clandestine gossip, grief. My sources remained secret, thereby establishing my reputation as scandal-monger extraordinaire. I was the first to broadcast the tell-all truth of our town's miseries in the girl's bathroom at school; smug, regal, it was the only way I knew to deflect attention from my own.

"Jim, it's Pete. Pete Sullivan. Sorry to be calling so late."

While my father prepared himself for what he knew he must hear, both ends were silent except for the squeaks of his mattress as he sat up, click of a light switch, rustle of paper. My father, a lawyer, took notes of these calls on a legal pad due to the potential negligence of his middle-of-the-night attention, in order to relay the information without additions or subtractions. The crumpled yellow wads covered with his black scrawl were then stuffed into the back of his top dresser drawer, alongside my mother's stationary, junk jewelry, unused panty-hose, credit cards, long overdue library books, and outdated identification cards.

"What's wrong?" My father's voice was now clear and clipped of sleep.

"The Conroys' daughter disappeared."

A pause, then my father said, "Which one?"

"Jessica."

"But she's only thirteen. She's Kathleen's age for Chrissakes. Did she leave a note before she took off?   Hints as to where she might go?"

"She didn't run." A long pause, then, "She was taken." Mr. Sullivan spoke slowly, tentatively, as if saying it might make it worse or make it true.

"From what Kathleen tells me, the Conroys give their kids a pretty free rein."

My neck prickled at the sound of my name and I waited for Mr. Sullivan to say something about me, that I was smart or pretty or talented.

Instead, he said, "She was out walking the dog at Wiley Pond. Kristi thinks it was around nine or ten o'clock when she left. But she wasn't sure since she didn't actually see Jessica leave, only heard the dog's nails scratching across the floor and the front door slamming shut. Around two this morning, some kids were out at the pond drinking beer, screwing around, the usual. They found the dog on the far side of the parking area. Run over. The leash was still attached."

"Jesus Christ," my father said, then, "Fuck. Goddamn. Fuck."

I was scared of my father's voice, a strange, ugly, twisted thing. I wanted to hang up on it but couldn't because then he would know I'd been listening all along.

But Mr. Sullivan had nothing else to say since there really wasn't anything else. Nobody had seen anything or heard anything. Nothing was left behind but the dog, which, by initial reports, looked deliberately run over, not struck, because its head had been crushed.

They hung up.

My father thumped around in his room. I listened to the silent phone, afraid to move, but then my father picked up again and there was the rapid click of dialing numbers, then nothing, then my father's voice: "Hello? Pete? You still there?"

I hung up quickly and flipped to my stomach, face mashed into the pillow, heart pounding, and arms crossed beneath me, trying to hold it all together.

Taken. I saw taken kids on the backs of milk cartons, with the wide, forced smiles of the yearly school photo, eyes focused right through the absent camera, at me. Always kids. I'd looked for my mother there, even though she was dead and I had seen her dressed up in her coffin, beautiful and cold and content. But I didn't like to think of her dead, or dying, because I couldn't imagine it, wouldn't remember to believe that her leaving had been deliberate, and so I looked for her everywhere. My father did this, too; sometimes if we were in a restaurant or at a store and I was talking, he would look over me, scanning the room, the women, trying to hear her voice, see her face, her gestures in the others.

I hoped Mrs. Conroy had a good photo. Jessica hated last year's; she had just gotten braces soldered across her teeth and refused to smile or say "cheeseburger." She had left her hair unbrushed and her kinky red hair, normally frizzled in tight, hot iron curls, had mushroomed into a wiry cloud. Right before the picture, she sneaked to the bathroom, lined her eyelids navy blue and colored her lips orange. I was in line after her and watched as she stalked back into the dark classroom with its shades drawn all the way to the floor. She arranged herself on the stool, looked right out into the hot bright light, and said, "Get it over with." The photographer came at her with a miniature pink brush, hand poised to attempt something with her hair, but she glared at him, flashed a silver sneer, and said, "Don't you dare touch me. My mother wants the picture, not me." He retreated behind his camera, brush tucked into his back pocket, and snapped her picture without another word.

The open door cracked light across the bed and my father hovered in the doorway. I knew he was wondering whether or not I needed to be awakened and told. If he had to tell me at all. Though he didn't move, breathe even, I heard him. The room seemed to buckle beneath his waiting.

"Kathleen," he whispered. "Are you up?"

We waited.

"Kathleen." He was over me then, with a hand on my back, light now, weightless, not really even there. "Kathy, honey." Tap tap tap.

I twitched, kicked, shook my head into the pillow, then opened my eyes slowly.

"What? What is it?" I grumbled, pulling my head out of the pillow.

"It's okay. Go back to sleep. I thought I heard you calling me." He tucked the sheet over my shoulders, kissed his fingers, touched them to the top of my head, and left, closing the door so quietly behind him it was as if he had never come in.

He went downstairs to the kitchen to call the Hausers, the final phone call to end the chain. The microwave beeped on, beeped off. I smelled coffee. Finally, after a few minutes, there was the rise and fall of his voice, the only sound in the house that I'd been staying awake to hear. I crept to the middle of the stairs. Not to listen, but to see, to reassure myself that it was still my father, that he wasn't going to disappear. He was facing the sliding doors, the backyard, the dark, talking to the Hausers without his notes, and never came back to bed.

Then it was morning, Sunday, June 22nd, the second day of Jessica Conroy's disappearance.

Her *disappearance.* That's what we said, meaning: ceased to be visible, passed from sight. But also implying: reappearance. Disappear. Reappear. A reversible state of being performed by Wally the Great, every February on our gym stage during the magazine pep rally. Out of the audience Wally picked, from a sea of waving hands, the kid pushed to the back row or far-end aisle seat in the competitive jostling for prime positions. The chosen one floated quickly down a side aisle, tripped once or twice on the newly waxed floor, and rose to the stage, blushing, nervous, ablaze in the glory of Wally's attention. We watched enviously as the chosen one promised never to reveal the secret of disappearance, and after a final wave goodbye, stepped inside the closet. With a swoop of his wand, Wally performed the disappearance; with the rap of his white-gloved hand, he performed the reappearance and sent the chosen one back to the audience clutching a Mini-Magic kit.

Nothing really bad had ever happened in our town, a safe haven for upper-middle-class lawyers and doctors, bankers and traders, and their valuables, which were: children, custom golf clubs, sailboats and a happiness willfully ignorant of the senseless crimes that occurred beyond our borders, places whizzed through in the comparative safety of the railroad's commuter cars. Car theft, break-ins, residential speeders, and high school keg parties were the kinds of crimes that were handled by the police.

But it was as if the town emptied out overnight in anticipation of disaster. I didn't wake to the predictable whine of lawn mowers gunning up at 7 A.M., or cars rolling out of driveways for town, then returning with the required bagels and Sunday *Times,* to parents trotting alongside their baby joggers, huffing and puffing up our hill or my father leaving for an 8 A.M. tee off, sticking twenty bucks on my dresser for the movies, the beach, whatever. Instead, lawns remained unmown for the weekend, dandelions topped out over the scraggly cascade of green, and the air hovered heavy and hot without the clean smell of sheared grass. The bagel bakery, which usually buzzed with a line snaking out to the sidewalk, dumped five trash bags crammed with end-of-the day bagels in the dumpster. Out-of-doors exercise was deemed vulgar, flip, and people secretly aerobicized in basements. My father took me to church, which was unusually crowded for the 10 A.M. Mass.

The born-again Catholics were packed fifteen and twenty to a pew or stood braced against sidewalks, fanning themselves with missalettes, squeezing eyes shut in prayer, kneeling without slouching or resting their butts on the pews. The Sign of Peace took ten minutes: people clamored to shake hands with as many neighbors as possible, and Father Rooney shuffled up and down the aisles grasping at hands, swinging incense, flicking holy water, and signing the cross over our heads. We wanted a magician and a priest. He sensed this, knew that we weren't there for the Word of God or his homily, but for the blessing.

After Mass, the parking lot flooded with the faithful. Police cars buzzed around, squawked their lights once or twice, startling us with the menace. It was agreed that children wouldn't be allowed on the search. Father Rooney opened up the basement, and everyone not over sixteen trudged down after him, and for five hours played dodge ball and board games missing most of their pieces, watched *Mary Poppins*, gossiped.

Those of us too old to play, too young to search, sat in a powwow in the corner, sipping slushy orange drink and eating stale, half-frozen mini-donuts that Father Rooney found in the freezer. The powdered sugar flaked off in cold clumps

"I bet she's hanging out in the city with some guy."

"Maybe she's hitchhiking to California."

"My mom said she looked like she was using drugs."

"What if some psycho killer took her for a sex slave?"

"What if she's dead?"

"She can't be dead."

"She's dead" I finally said. "Dead." That shut them all up.

"You're such a liar, Kathy."

None of them seemed to know anything, so I said (proud to be the informer, the one who knew more than the rest of them), "Whoever took her crushed Fritzie's skull."

Lisa Michaels began to cry, then Gwen Hopper. Tommy Farinello raised his bushy eyebrows, Billy Mulryan gasped, "Holy Shit."

Stephanie Lewis glared at me. "You never know when to stop. This is real, not some stupid lie. Why would anyone want to kill that dumb dog?" She stalked off.

I shrugged and looked at all of them, one by one in the eye. "I don't care if you don't believe me. But she's dead. I

know that she is. I know about these things." I dare you, I
wanted to say, I dare you to say that I don't.

One by one they left and played team Monopoly in the
far corner. Nobody spoke to me after that. But I didn't care
what they thought. I can't lie about the dead.

Every morning, for a week straight, the commuter
train pulled away from the station loaded with college
graduates heading off to new jobs, the elderly for their
doctor's appointments in Manhattan, and the few, the very
few, childless couples off to work. The rest stayed home to
search.

New rules, the first statute:

I twirled into the kitchen in my new bikini, a modest
two-piece, no strings or push-up underwire. "What do you
think?"

My father was sorting through a stack of crinkled faxes,
and without even really looking at me, said, "You're too
young. Go up and change."

I stomped upstairs to change out of my new suit, just
bought with my own money I'd earned from babysitting at
the pool, into an old, faded Speedo racerback. I scowled
upon my return; he nodded in approval.

"Mom would have let me wear it. Besides, I know not
to take candy and rides from strangers. And in case you
didn't notice, there are locks on the windows and doors,
and a working alarm system. And I know how to kick a guy
where it hurts." I bit my lower lip, trying not to smile, and
said, "In the balls. I could kick him in the balls. See?" Fists
clenched to my sides, I chopped my leg into the air, kicking
at a height I imagined would suffice.

He looked up from the paper, eyes gray and red from
too much coffee, too little sleep. "Humor me, Kathleen."

I scraped the chair back from the table and sat down. "This is idiotic. He'd be stupid to come back here with the parent brigade patrolling the streets." I stabbed my spoon at a bowl of soggy Lucky Charms.

"I'd rather be on the safe side. A lot can happen in a couple of hours. Even in a minute. And you never know. He could come back here, he knows the area. Maybe he lives here. We just don't know." His voice tightened at the last words, like he was closing something off, some thought he didn't want to think.

"Maybe she's in some secret hole in somebody's basement. That doesn't sound so bad to me." And it hadn't a couple of years before when it happened to a girl from the South Shore. Her neighbor built an underground room, complete with cable, and kept her there for two weeks before the police found out. He installed Nintendo, stocked a mini fridge with soda and candy, cooked her favorite meals, and emptied the makeshift toilet twice a day. He told the police he was protecting her, from her parents, from the beatings they gave her which he heard from his house next door, from the world. He didn't hurt her, ever, she said, and he let her watch whatever she wanted on television. That hadn't sounded too terrible.

"Don't you dare say that again," he said, his voice quiet, measuring out each word. "This is one of your friends."

I knew he was angry, really angry, but I couldn't stop myself. "Acquaintance. She was a bad influence, remember?"

The year before, Jessica mailed out thirty invitations marked, "Sssshhhh! Surprise Party! For Jessica! Regrets Only: Patty Conroy, 425-9708." That was Jessica's own private line which connected to her own private answering machine. Nineteen boys and girls managed to lie to their parents, aided by the official notice, and drank vodka punch, made out in her parents' bedroom, then threw up in toilets, on carpets, in the front seats of cars when they were picked up at 11 P.M. My father held my hair back as I threw up in our driveway, then grounded me for a month, with the added clause that I could be friendly, but not friends, with Jessica.

"That doesn't change anything. You're my daughter. I'm your father. No room for argument. Until I can be sure that you're safe, you've got yourself a chauffeur."

"What if we never know? Maybe she's gone for good. Fucking forever. Maybe she hates her fucking parents and doesn't want to come back." I was shouting now and didn't care, using words I'd never used in front of him, directing them intentionally at him. I was angry and scared at the same time.

He slammed his palm on the table, catching the edge of my cereal bowl, which flipped, spraying a puddle of marshmallows and milk on the floor, on me, on him.

"Kathleen," he said, "clean up this mess and let's go."

"It's your mess. Not mine. I'm not the one throwing things around."

He stood up with his hand opened up flat and I shrank into the seat, away from him. Face red, drops of milk in his hair, a large wet spot on his shirt. He looked ridiculous, like an ogre or Blue Beard, ready to knock off my head. But his hand fell to his side, heavy and stiff, and he just looked confused and sad like he must have after Mr. Sullivan's phone call, after finding my mother.

He walked out the kitchen door and stood in the middle of the patio, not moving at all, just staring out at nothing, at the empty flowerbeds and flower barrels, the rusted wrought-iron furniture and their faded cushions, at a table umbrella that was bent and couldn't be raised.

Except for the lawn manicured by the Morelli Brothers, our neighborhood landscapers, our backyard was abandoned. All across town, lawns blended seamlessly into each other, and you could walk across the sea of green—lawn to lawn to lawn, all around town, cutting through backyards and side yards, leapfrogging across streets via middle-of-the-road islands decorated with begonias, impatiens, and shrubs sheared into perfect circles—without ever leaving the safety of grass except to cross the two main avenues. That was why my parents moved here when I learned to walk.

Suddenly my father charged across the yard like a linebacker, shoulders and head hunched near the ground, towards the tall pine. No, at it. I pressed my face into the glass yelling for him to stop, wanting to throw myself in front of him, but he couldn't hear me, and it didn't matter because he leaped into the air and smacked the long, plastic-tube birdfeeder that hung empty with his hand. It reeled once around the branch, tangled on its second loop, swayed to a stop. He grabbed it again, this time hurling it at the trunk like a torpedo. It shattered. He bent over and picked up a few of the larger pieces, tried to fit them together, wondering, I knew, if it could be repaired with superglue, but finally gave up.

My father bought a fax machine so that he could work from home until Jessica reappeared. What he told me was that he wanted to help a few hours a day in the search, canvassing the neighborhood, answering phones at the after-school room of the library, now the official Jessica Conroy Command Center. I knew he didn't want to leave me alone to chance. I could no longer bike to friends' houses or the Yacht Club where I had spent every summer previous, swimming, sailing, and running up a large chit at the snack bar for hamburgers, french fries, and ice cream bars.   He now drove me every morning, waited until I had signed in, then picked me up again in the afternoon, insisting that I remain inside the gates where the attendant could see me. He dragged me to the nightly Update meetings, where I, along with virtually every other under-sixteen-year old, could stay under the watchful eyes of geriatric librarians.

I tried calling friends, pulled my phone into the closet and shut myself inside.   It was easier in there, hidden in a pile of dirty laundry and the long dangling dresses and skirts, to be hung up on.   I didn't really have a best friend, but like a nomad, migrated in and out of friendships.   So there was no one who was loyal to me, who would tell people to "Fuck off," or try to explain why I said the things I did.   After four calls, four "I'm not talking to you...I heard what you said about Jessica...You're a sick bitch...Maybe you killed her," I quit.   I was the new pariah and curled up on top of my shoes, hoped I would die.

My father was a zombie.   A typical evening after a search: drink scotch at five, pass out on the couch by seven, wake up at ten, startled, bleary-eyed, embarrassed, not meaning to get drunk, to pass out.   I napped in the closet, the darkest place I could find to get away from the long summer light.

Neither of us could sleep at night.   But we weren't awake together.   My father paced the downstairs, dictated memorandums for a lawsuit and letters to clients into a palm-sized recorder.   He would start and stop and start and rewind and start all over again: *To: Morgan Dulles From: Jim Dillon Re: Dulles Manufacturing v Ikado Corp. Stop.   To: John DiBella, Pres.   From: Jim Dillon Re: State of*

*New York v Technology Unlimited, Inc. Stop. To: Margaret
Dillon From: James Dillon Re: The Non-negotiable Terms of
Your Death. Rewind.*

I remained in bed, flopped on top of the sheets, sweating.
Then it would start. First, I imagined what it must have
been like to disappear, if Jessica saw the car approaching
and tried to run, or if he crept up from behind, pounced on
her dog, then her. If he taped her mouth and tied her hands
and threw her into his trunk. I placed a sock across my
mouth, clasped my hands under the small of my back, and
heard the car crunching over gravel, gliding down the streets
of our neighborhood, saw it circling in and out of cul-de-
sacs, taunting us: how easy, how easy and how stupid you
all are. I moaned, beat my heels into the mattress, rolled my
head from side to side. *Help,* I thought, *help me.* Nothing.

This led to my imagining her dead. No matter how
I tried to stop the thought from coming, it came, swiftly,
surely. Jessica, naked in the woods, neck broken. Jessica,
naked in an attic, heart stabbed. Jessica, naked in water,
body bloated. My mother, nightgowned in bed, dead.
Four empty canisters of pills by her side that were supposed
to help postpartum depression, return her happiness, but
the new baby was dead, dead at birth, dead from the very
moment his little head emerged from her body. They were
wrong about it being hormonal, about it being something
she could eventually, if not forget, forgive herself for. My
mother blamed her body, the drinking water on Long Island,
a glass of wine in the early weeks of pregnancy, her weekly
tennis game, a high pollen count, poisonous microbes, and
ultimately and only herself.

So my mother, safe because I was at school, takes the
pills mid-morning, calls my father at work: *You need to
pickup Kathleen from school and drop her off at gymnastics.*

I can't. Please, I'll explain later. He leaves work at two, drops me off to cartwheels and somersaults by three, finds her comatose at four. By the time I had finished walking the balance beam at five, my mother's stomach had been pumped, her heart stopped, her brain dead.

After the first week, after walking five abreast through backyards and undeveloped plots of land, after German shepherds sniffed through the tall weedy grass around the edge of the pond and the County police in scuba gear mucked their way through it, turning up nothing, the police decided that there was nothing else the town could do, that it was time to go back to living our lives, to trust them. Parents flocked to the Command Center, along with various town officials. It was the last night of the last search, and they were defeated.

On the ride over, my father cried, and I didn't know what to do with his grief, how to comfort him, just looked out the window into night, needing him to stop. All children under the age of sixteen were herded upstairs into the adult section by Mrs. Flanders and the PAL police officer for a refresher course in self-defense. Before my father relinquished my arm (he gripped it so tightly over the past few days whenever I made a move to separate—as if touch alone convinced him I was there, not missing—that there was a row of faint blue fingerprints on my arm), I saw Mr. and Mrs. Conroy seated at a front table. As they watched parents squishing into the orange, plastic chairs, I wondered what they wanted, besides search parties and hope and prayers, if they thought that it was one of us, one of our fathers or brothers who had driven up to Jessica and offered her the ride.

Above the tabletop, the Conroys were still, severed statues, silenced by the stack of flyers between them. Below the table? A jitter of tapping feet, and hands clenching and unclenching, reaching for each other, squeezing, then letting go.

"Dad," I said, "can't I stay? I'll learn more here. It's not like they can teach me anything I don't know already." It was a good hook. My father, never one to waste an educational opportunity, turned even the mundane trips to the movies into a learning experience: fourteen tickets times fifteen people? Add three seniors, one under five equals? Subtitles in French, German, and Japanese. Absurd lessons, like the stupid slogans in health class: *This is your brain on drugs. Only abstinence makes the heart grow fonder. You don't get a second chance with suicide.* As if any of us believed them.

Besides, upstairs I knew that I would be shunned, by friends, by not-friends, stuck with myself.

He scanned the room, tugged his chin, and shook his head at the same time. "I don't think it's a good idea. There aren't any other kids so maybe the Conroys need it this way.

"I'm not a kid," I said, and pushed away from him, elbow in ribs. "I've heard worse."

His face broke open, and he made a move to hug me.

"Don't," I said. "Don't." His arms dropped, hung empty. I left him standing outside the doors decorated with red, white, and blue construction paper flags and yellow pipe cleaner fireworks, and walked upstairs to learn from my PAL Officer Mike how to protect myself from strangers, and sometimes, even, family.

Instead of watching Officer Mike attack Mrs. Flanders, who blew a plastic whistle, screamed, then stubbed him gently in the kneecap with her clunky brown shoe, I wandered into the Romance racks, daydreamed about a dark, handsome stranger kidnapping me, making me his child bride. Jessica's brother and sister huddled together in the magazine room, flipping through *Sports Illustrated* and *Glamour*, detached from the circle of new recruits, from the hysteria around them, as if they knew something the rest of us didn't. I'd heard one of the searchers tell my father that the Conroys were making a family effort, putting on a united front.

Jessica was always complaining to us at lunchtime how much she hated her parents, how they couldn't care less about any of them, except when it came to the Christmas card photo when they all had to wear matching red (for the boys) and green (for the girls) sweaters, and sprawl like a pack of dogs in front of a roaring fireplace in August. We didn't give her complaints much notice—after all, her parents bought kegs of beer for monthly parties thrown by Scott, a senior at our school; her older sister, Kristi, took her to concerts at Madison Square Garden; and they all went to St. Croix for Christmas, returning bronzed and happy to snow and school. Maybe Jessica was camped out nearby, basking in the whirlwind of attention, teaching her parents a thing or two about love, or she had gone willingly with a gruff, handsome stranger who would teach her about love.

I didn't want to believe what I felt to be true. I wanted to hope that she was okay. That it was a trick. But I couldn't get my mind around the dog. She loved that dog. It was hers.

The police finally made the last official door-to-door rounds of the neighborhood, questioning parents that they had seen every day at the command center, cleaning ladies who never cleaned at night, even little kids, asking if they saw anything, heard anything that night, expecting to find out nothing. They finally got to our house.

I recognized the officer because he had been in our living room four years ago and my father and I answered their questions, their stupid, awful questions, while a matched pair were upstairs looking through my mother's things. I hated him. I told him so. My father seemed to also, and I didn't have to apologize.

It had changed: my father now called him Pat, and Pat called him Jim, and it wasn't the living room, but the den, and my father poured coffee and I had to make sandwiches, pour a bag of chips into a bowl. The Yankees were on television, and they swapped statistics on players.

Officer Pat smiled at me between bites of his sandwich, bobbing his head up and down, like a dumb buoy. "Not hungry? Aww, c'mon. You made these great sandwiches and you're not even going to sample your own creation?"

I glared back.

He leaned over across the armrest and nudged my father. "Since when is Kathleen at a loss for words?"

My father didn't flash the warning; his face stayed loose, his voice stayed even, he laughed. I wanted to punch both of them. Instead I said, "I saw a white pickup following her a few weeks ago, you know."

My father stopped laughing and Officer Pat sat up straight, stunned, then looked at my father.

"Kathleen," my father said, "what are you talking about? You haven't said anything about this before." I could tell he didn't believe me but Officer Pat did. He dropped his second sandwich, swallowed a mouthful of unchewed chips, and coughed.

I shrugged. "I didn't think it was anything. It might not be since it was weeks before she disappeared."

Officer Pat was writing every word I said onto a little pad of paper; his hand jerked back and forth, trying to catch up. Out of the corner of my eye I saw my father waiting, watching me carefully. I ignored him.

"I was walking home and she was walking home, but not together. I was a block behind her."

"When?"

"I'd have to check my class schedule. I don't really remember."

My father gripped my shoulder, his thumb pressed hard. "Go get it, Kathleen," he said, angry now. "Why didn't you tell me this a week ago? Why would you keep this to yourself?"

I shrugged his hand off. "You're hurting me."

"Jim, don't be so hard on her. Kids don't always remember when we need them to remember," Officer Pat said.

"The pickup was white. It wasn't new. Old. I couldn't really get a good look at it. But it passed me and slowed up by Jessica, followed beside her to the corner. I figured it was a friend of her brother or sister. I mean, she didn't run or anything."

Officer Pat was nodding. "What else?"

"There isn't anything else. It turned the corner and she kept walking on. It could have been anything. Someone lost or a friend, I don't know." I wanted to stop, but heard myself babble on. "But I thought it was strange, because no one we know owns pickups. I mean, nobody would be caught dead driving a pickup in this town. That's a hick truck. The only pickups I see around here belong to landscaping guys."

Officer Pat raised his eyebrows, his pen barely keeping up with my words. "Okay, Kathleen. Why don't you check your schedule so I can get an exact date?" He paused and touched my hand, thanking me I supposed. "If this is something, Kathleen, you're lucky." He was saying this to me, but he was looking at my father, saying, without saying it, that he was lucky the pickup didn't stop for me.

I got away with the lie.

For the rest of the week, we stuck to an unofficial cease-fire, retreating into our own corners, not daring to cross paths unless absolutely necessary, and even then we maintained a strained civility. I hovered outside the kitchen, waiting for my father to finish his morning coffee; he puttered around the fax machine, waiting for me to finish my breakfast. I stuffed myself at the club and bowed out of dinner; he forgot to eat without me. When I first took on the responsibility of dinner after my mother was gone, I staged the elaborate recipes circled or underlined in her battered cookbooks, Citrus-Crusted Shrimp, Roast Pork Tenderloin, Curried Silken Chicken, then fell back on my father's favorites, baked chicken, spaghetti, hamburgers, Campbell's Soup. I didn't mind the repetitive menu since we both agreed nothing tasted good anymore.

But I worried now. For five entire days, he ate peanuts, pretzels, and bagels, drank only coffee and scotch.

Television rescued us; we didn't have to talk to each other, but could talk around each other, about the things that flashed in front of us. We sat at opposite ends of the room; he slumped in the recliner, I stretched out on the couch. The coffee table was equidistant, so no awkward bumping of hands when passing potato chips or the remote control since it was all within an arm's length of the both of us.

Friday evening: he looked at his watch, then flipped the channels quickly back to the five o'clock news, then leaned forward expectantly, as he always did, waiting for news of Jessica. But this time her parents were on television, sitting in their living room on the piano bench pulled in front of the fireplace. They looked awful, shell-shocked in the television screen. My father didn't seem to notice any difference, but then he saw them every day, witnessing their decline up close.

The camera zoomed in on Mrs. Conroy, then closer, on her empty gaze projected into our living room, at me. Her eyes were puffy and red, but not as if she had just cried, as if she couldn't cry anymore, as if there was nothing left to give up. She wasn't wearing makeup and wrinkles I'd never seen winged out from her eyes and mouth, crossed her forehead. The camera panned to Mr. Conroy, zoomed closer on his arm wrapped around her shoulders, then pulled back to show them together, united. For an instant, her body crumpled and his arm jolted, drew her tight to his side, holding her up. Behind them, on the mantle, a row of pictures, large eight-by-tens, all of them of Jessica, last year's school photo.

"Please," began Mrs. Conroy, "please return our daughter, Jessica." She turned to her husband, who was still now except for his lips which were pressed together, trembling, chewing on his grief, keeping it in. "Jessica means everything to us. Jessica needs to be home with her family, with her father."

As if on cue, Mr. Conroy turned to the camera, blinked twice, grinding his jaw back and forth, then looked back at his wife. "She needs to be home with her mother, her brother and sister who love her and miss her very much."

The camera panned to Kristi and Scott on the couch, the same vacant faces gaping into the camera. Then, from the background, Mr. Conroy said, "Give her back, you bastard."

Even though they were devastated, falling apart in front of the world, they held each other together. I was jealous, yes, sick with jealousy, but trampled and buried underneath that, ashamed.

Later that night, after my father fell asleep on the couch, I biked over to Wiley Pond. He wouldn't drive me past the spot because he didn't think I needed to see it or think about it. That didn't make any sense. After all, we hadn't abandoned our house. Besides, death didn't scare me, not anymore.

I hid my bike behind a tree so none of the roaming patrol cars would see it, and walked the path around the pond. It was the first time I wasn't under watch in what felt like years. A large area was still roped off with yellow police tape that stretched from tree to tree to tree to tree, a magic square warding off the curse of the crime scene. I ducked underneath and looked across the pond, across a row of trees, to our house somewhere in the distance, locked up tight. I knelt and pressed my hand into the dirt, trying to feel some trace of her, feel where it went wrong, but felt nothing. Just the damp ground. I prayed that she would forgive me for my lie, that it wouldn't hurt her. I touched my fingers to my lips, rubbed dirt across them, hoped the curse would rub off on me.

Later that week, Officer Pat and some other man dressed in an ugly dark suit, the kind that funeral directors liked so much, showed up at our house again. My father was out in the backyard on his hands and knees digging up weeds in the flower beds. He had returned from the garden center earlier in the day, and instead of a trunk filled with flats of begonias or impatiens, he had a large sack filled with seed packets: daisies, pansies, purple asters.

He fanned a few packets in his hand and waved them at me. "A royal flush," he said, and smiled, proud to finally be doing something that might make the house a home again. "Try to beat this hand of happiness."

"You can't be that dumb," I said, trying to sound light. "Didn't you ever pay attention to what Mom did? She bought them already grown. You plant flowers, Dad, not seeds." I laughed, needing to ruin this for him, but didn't know why, only knew that I felt ugly and mean.

He rubbed his thumb back and forth across the bottoms of the packets, then folded, and set the stack on the table. "You win, Kathleen, I'm out. Your stakes are too high."

But he didn't fold after all; for two hours he had been out back, digging out weeds, tamping in seeds, ignoring me. I was stretched out on a lounge chair reading a book, trying to not talk to him, to remain silent at an intentional remove.

But then Officer Pat showed up with the weird quiet man. I pointed them over to my father and yelled, "Dad."

He didn't turn around, just jammed the spade deep into the ground. "Yeah, Kathleen, I know. I'm stupid for doing this."

"No, Dad. Some people are here to see you."

He turned around, then rocked back into a squat and wiped his arm across his forehead, streaking dirt in its wake. I could see he was hot and tired but most of all sad, not angry anymore, just emptied out because of me.

"Pat."

"Sorry to disturb you. Gardening?"

My father shrugged, and waved his hand at the pile of mangled weeds heaped by his feet. "Trying to anyway. What can I do for you?"

"Not for me, Jim. For Federal Agent Pintowski. And you can't do it. We need Kathleen."

My father stood up, looked over at me, then back at the weird guy who was staring at me. I held my book up, shielded my face from them, pretended to read.

"What do you need Kathleen for?"

Officer Pat placed a hand on his hip and I imagined him feeling his gun, wondering if he should just shoot me

right then and there for lying to the police. But he said,
"One of our guys spotted a white pickup over on Highdale
Lane, a Mexican mowing the lawn. And Agent Pintowski
here has started working with us on this, and wanted to
come along to meet Kathleen, and to drive her by this guy
and his pickup. See if she can identify him."

I closed my eyes and waited for my father to stop them,
to tell them I'd lied, to leave us alone. In the distance, a
lawn mower whirred, not the Mexican's, but it might as well
have been because my hands started shaking.

But my father didn't say what I wanted him to say. He
just shrugged and said, "I guess that'll be okay. Just let me
get cleaned up and we'll be ready to go in a few minutes."

Agent Pintowski's voice cut in. "If it's all the same to
you, sir, I'd like to run your daughter by him alone. There's
less of a possibility of outside influence in the process."

I lowered the book an inch, and saw my father standing
in front of them, his jaw rigid, hands squared on his hips. "If
it's all the same to you, I think I'll go along for the ride. If
Kathleen has to see this guy, I want to make sure he doesn't
see her first, or even at all. This is my daughter we're talking
about, here. Not someone else's missing one."

Agent Pintowski made a move to say something but
Officer Pat raised his hand and nodded. "That's fine, Jim.
But you'll have to stay quiet. We don't want to be accused
of tampering with a potential witness."

When my father got into the backseat of the plain
brown car that sat at the bottom of our driveway I had no
choice but to follow him.

We drove slowly down Highdale Lane towards a white
pickup. A lawn mower was sitting up in its bed. Officer
Pat, sitting in the passenger side up front, rolled down his
window. I could hear the high whine of a weed whacker
close by.

"Good," Agent Pintowski said, "this is it. He must be around back. This will give you a chance to get a good look at the vehicle. Take your time, Miss Dillon."

The window on my side suddenly slid down as the car slowed to a stop. I wanted to puke. The white pickup was right next to us; I could have reached out and placed my palm flat against its side. A handprint that could be used for evidence. We inched by, and I saw every splotch of dirt, every dent, every finger smudge on the driver's window. For a moment, I tried to believe that the smudges were Jessica's, from her hands clutching for the door, trying to smash the glass. It took forever to get to the front end of the pickup, and all the while my father's hand was circled around my forearm, squeezing tight.

When we finally rolled to a stop at the end of the street, I turned to my father, wanted to cry.

He closed his eyes and nodded, then opened them. "You don't have to."

"Mr. Dillon," Agent Pintowski said, his voice hard, "No talking. Only Kathleen." He parked, and we listened to the car idle and the weed whacker whine, until finally the weed whacker stopped.

Officer Pat twisted around in his seat, his eyes moving from my face to the back window, at what was behind us.

My breath was short and choppy and sweat beaded in my armpit then slid down into my bra.

"It's him," Officer Pat said. "Our guy."

Agent Pintowski poked Officer Pat in the arm, and shook his head furiously at him.

"I mean," Officer Pat corrected, "there's the driver of the pickup."

He was Mexican or Guatemalan or Nicaraguan. Brown instead of white. Worker not resident. Outsider not insider.

Goggles covered his eyes, the weed whacker was slung over his shoulder, black hair was matted with sweat. He slid the goggles to the top of his head, walked to the side of the truck, opened the door, and pulled a wadded towel and a jug from the front seat. He mopped his forehead, the back of his neck, and then tilted the jug up to his mouth. I watched his Adam's apple bob up and down as he swallowed. Even though there had been no white pickup, and I had never seen him before, I tried to feel that maybe he could have taken Jessica. It could have been him as well as anyone else, and thousands of people can be suspects and then one day they're not suspects anymore because the real criminal gets caught.

But he looked so tired and hot and nice, like a gardener who planted flowers, like someone's father, someone who wouldn't know, didn't need to know about any of this, about me and my lie. Someone who didn't need to be haunted by some dead girl's disappearance. Who would work himself to death trying to give his wife and children a happy and peaceful life in a new country. But who would not die from work, but die as an old man surrounded by his wife, children, grandchildren, with the knowledge that he had lived a good and honorable life.

I closed the window, sealing us away from him. My father covered his face with his hands, dreading what I was about to say.

The men up front waited for me to throw them their bone.

"It's not him," I said, my voice quiet but then louder. "There isn't a him or a white pickup. Only me and a lie. I'm guilty. Not him."

My father dropped his hands in his lap, started to reach for me, but I shrank away.

Agent Pintowski was furious, and without even looking at me, said, "Young lady, I could arrest you for this, obstructing justice, tampering with an investigation, but I'll let you live with the fact that you have wasted precious time that could be devoted to the recovery of Jessica Conroy." He glanced at my father in the rearview mirror, and continued, "You sir, should have a talk with your daughter about the truth. Especially when it involves matters of life and death." Then, turning to Officer Pat, said, "And you, sir, should learn something about the proper interrogation of a witness."

I watched the back of Officer Pat's ears and neck flush a bright burning red. I wanted to cover his ears with my hands until he was no longer ashamed for having believed in me, a liar, a kid. I wanted to whisper into his ears so no one could hear: *It's not your fault. How could you interrogate me if I was never a witness?*

We were dropped off at our curb, neither officer saying good-bye, just staring ahead at the sea of manicured lawns that swelled up and down the street. My father retreated to the flower beds, and I to my room. For a long time, what seemed like years, but what was only a day, we didn't talk. The assigned lecture was never given.

Then it was the Fourth of July. Independence Day. The town seemed hopeful, my father, suddenly hungry.

"A barbecue would be nice," he said. "Restore some normalcy to the summer."

The grill hadn't been used since my mother disappeared from us, had stood guard outside the back door, waiting for summer, any kind of summer, to return.

"Dad, why go to the trouble for two? Can't we just burn some hotdogs on the stove?"

"That's not the point. It's the Fourth of July. We barbecue even if it's a lot of trouble. It's worth it." He tossed a legal pad and a pen at me. "Let's make a list."

Six grocery bags later, a new tank of propane, and it was as if my father, without warning, remembered something that he was determined to bring back. He could have thrown a barbecue for the entire block if he wanted. At the supermarket, he waved Ring Dings, a family pack of hamburger meat, bags of candy, cartons of ice cream, ten ears of corn at me. I shook my head but whatever was in his hands, whatever else he grabbed from the shelves, he tossed into the cart. He bowled rolls of paper towels, juggled bags of cookies and cans of baked beans, yelling from down the aisle, "Heads up!" I made no move to catch anything and left a trail of bags and dented cans in our wake.

"Invite some of your friends," he said. He was squatting next to the barbecue, under the hot noon sun, switching the tanks. I was sitting on the back stoop, shaded by the overhang, watching his folly. He looked up at me, sweaty, happy, and expectant, a man ready to stage a barbecue bonanza.

I shrugged. "No one to invite."

"C'mon Kathleen, there's got to be some kids around." He took a swig of his beer, wiped his forehead with his arm, grunting as he stood and straightened his back. "Abracadabra," he said and pushed the button. The grill made a "whumph," and as he turned the dial, flames hissed up through the grate.

"Presto," he said, and draped his arm across my shoulder, jostled me back and forth. "That wasn't so hard."

"Get off," I said, shimmying out from under him. "You're all sweaty."

"Don't be such a pain in the ass, Kathleen. Call up some friends. You've turned into a first-class mope, you know." He tried to laugh, trying to get me to give way.

"Why don't you call your police buddies? Or the Conroys. I'm sure they're in town with nothing better to do except wait for a phone call that's never going to come. Isn't that what we've been doing? Waiting for nothing, for no one? Jessica's dead. Mom's dead. D-E-A-D." I watched for the stumble, the twitch, needing him to hurt.

He moved his mouth before speaking, as if testing out the words before speaking them aloud. "Kathleen, I know I've been a jerk. I'm sorry for that. But these few weeks searching, hoping, they've been for you. I can't imagine what it would be like for you to disappear on me, all at once, without warning. To disappear and not know if you were ever coming back."

He kicked the empty tank; it rolled across the patio, and knocked over a stack of empty flower boxes. He sighed and leaned against the house, arms braced against the wall, head hanging, eyes closed. A runner's stretch, only instead of bolting in a sprint down the block, he held steady. But then I saw that his fingers, splayed open against the bricks, and his arms, extended in rigid lines from shoulders to wrists, were trembling, pushing against the wall as if expecting the bricks to slide from the mortar, the house to collapse on its foundation, all of it, finally, to give way.

I hoped it would. Weren't we rubble anyway, with Jessica and my mom buried underneath?

But then he pushed off the wall and squatted at my feet, each hand holding a sneaker in place and said, "You want to know what I'm waiting for? Not for your mother to come back. She's dead, we know that for sure. Right? And your friend Jessica? Okay, fine. Probably dead, too, but maybe we'll never know. But I know this. What you've been doing, slowly disappearing, piece by piece? That scares me to death. If you go, I couldn't, wouldn't go on. So what I'm waiting for is you."

His hands tightened around my feet and as he leaned in closer, I saw that his eyes were red and wet, the skin underneath sagging, his face, usually tan by now from Saturday golf games, was blotchy and pale and his hair, trimmed every other week in a neat cap around his head, was shaggy. He looked sick or old or maybe just sad.

That scared me so I turned away, picked at a scab on my knee, refused to look back at him, and said slowly, measuring my words, "Sometimes I wish I was dead so I wouldn't have to be here with you, without her." I wanted to burn myself up in the grill, disappear into black ash.

He sighed, all his expectation emptying out, stood up and turned off the grill. The flames were gone, no smoke, no ash. "It's okay. I don't mind you hating me. But I don't want you to hate yourself. I won't let you." He leaned over, and because I was still watching the ground trying to hold myself steady, I didn't see it coming. He kissed my forehead, and whispered against it, "Kathleen, please."

When his lips left my forehead something inside me let go, anger uncurled, ashes swept away. I tried to think about my mother, gone now except for the orderly arrangement of bones in the family plot, her perfect white skeleton all that remained. I tried to think about Jessica, her bones tossed in a pile somewhere, the woods or a cardboard box. But I didn't want to. They weren't waiting for me.

And neither was the neighborhood. For one afternoon, it had forgotten its fear, in the holiday, in the resurrection of ritual, and while not exactly celebrating, was reprieved, whirring back to life in the monotonous, welcomed drone of lawn mowers and cicadas, children and families. Between us though, it was quiet, something was determined to exact change. It would have been so effortless and uncomplicated to have abandoned him to his own grief and refused him mine. But he was waiting for me and I knew I didn't want to be alone anymore with the dead and their dying

NECESSARY LIES

A t first you forget that she is pregnant at all, think in that half-asleep way that if you can wake her up without the coffee there might be time to make love, quickly. You open one eye to check the time, then remember and look at her instead. Her belly swells beneath a sheet twisted in folds around her body, a finger of damp hair curled around her neck, a daughter suspended inside her.

You think: nothing else matters but this.

I had been waking up like that for months now, watching Gwen grow and our daughter grow, losing more of the sheet every week to her. I didn't mind. I never liked covers anyway, but slept under them to be near her. This was necessary because we had a king-sized monstrosity, a wedding present from Gwen's mother, which got me wondering exactly how close she wanted us to be. She had imagined a heart surgeon or a Mergers-and-Acquisitions guy, somebody who would go big places, acquire big things besides debt. We accepted the bed graciously though, since ours was a cheap lumpy futon, bedrock that refused to give to our curves.

Nothing else matters except: "Whose is this?" Gwen asked over coffee, organic decaf, one morning. She was holding up a marbled notebook, a student journal, in one hand, and in the other, palmed a rainbow assortment of vitamins.

"Jill Casey's," I said and held out my hand for it. Jill had filled the white spaces in with black marker.

The journal was part of the grade. They could write about anything they wanted as long as it was in writing, a response in the standard alphabet. Most of the kids stuck to a standard diary format: *Monday, October 13. Fight with boyfriend. Fight with Mom. Fight with Dad.* Others took more time and relished the chance to describe their hidden lives, in detail, to an adult: *Got shitfaced Friday night and puked all over Henry in the backseat of Jimmy's car. Hooked up with Steven at Linda's party.* Others used the journals to respond to books we read in class, to throw me a quick one-two: *This book sucks and so do you.* But that was okay, I could take it. I told them it was neither my role to censor nor to approve.

Gwen liked to leaf through the journals because she wanted to know the kids that I taught, wanted to help me know them. She had majored in psychology as an undergrad at the State University, got her master's in industrial psych at NYU, and worked at New York National Bank's corporate headquarters in Human Resources. Mostly she interviewed or weeded out potential hirees, dealt with the first rounds of sexual harassment complaints, organized time and stress management seminars, counseled coworkers through illicit office romances. Occasionally her ingenuity was rewarded and integrated into corporate policy. Her latest coup: every Wednesday, a contingent of Ten-Minute Masseuses roamed the floors providing, as the name suggests, ten-minute rubdowns to needy, stressed-out employees with neck cramps and backaches. They didn't even have to leave their desks, just stretched forward in their rolling chairs and bowed their heads for the laying on of hands.

I was a little uncomfortable with Gwen's studious perusal; technically it was an invasion of my students' privacy, but she'd never meet the girls, never speak to them, unless, like a scout troop of Holden Caulfields, they showed up on the doorstep in the middle of the night.

She opened the notebook on the table and spun it around to face me. "Well, hon, Jill Casey is in trouble."

I looked down at the page covered in fat, cursive "i's" dotted with hearts. Okay, so the rest of the page was in blue ink and the hearts were in black, but it didn't really look like a girl in obvious trouble to me, just a little healthy adolescent angst. "She seems fine. Quiet, but that's not extraordinary."

Jill sat in the front row and blushed whenever I called on her. She was smart, perceptive, and loved to read. She asked me to draw up book lists for her, came back for new titles each week. She talked about literature, how it was beautiful and good and could change everything. But only outside of class; she never talked inside.

"Yeah, well, people are quiet on death marches, too. Do you even read what these kids write?" Gwen asked, lips pursed, shaking her head, dramatizing her disapproval. She had already decided against me.

"Look. You know I do, not every word, but most of them."

Gwen drummed her fingers on her stomach, and I wondered what the baby heard, felt—if its adrenaline rose with hers, if its tiny fingers drummed back *tap tap tap tap*. "I get it. You're trying to discover the next little Hemingway, the one who will make it all worthwhile. Read it," she demanded, banging her finger on top of the notebook, "because this one is looking for a shotgun, too."

So I read: *I wake up cold. I want to scream and scream but my voice is gone. No one cares. Not even me. Blah Blah Blah. Life can go on without me. It always has.*

"See," Gwen said. She was pressing her fingers down into the edge of the table, so hard the tips were turning white.

"I see. I see," I said.

She shook her head in disgust now.

"No, Gwen, hon, I do. So she's not writing about boys. She sounds like a normal teenager."

"Normally abnormal. Don't you dare turn your back on her, Mike. Don't you dare say it's normal, that it's a hyperbolic, histrionic developmental phase all hormonally charged teenage girls go through. Don't you dare do that. Everyone has probably done that to her." She pushed her mug away, reached for my hand, and held it tight against her chest. "Just talk to her, please" she said, "as if she were your own."

Gwen didn't let go of my hand, but held it close, wanting me to feel the echoes of the baby moving and then something deeper still inside.

When it came down to it, I still believed that the right words could save. Money. Time. Grief. Lives. And that I could say the right words at the right times. At least, that's what I told myself, ten years after switching from pre-med to English, from a belief in the perfect systems of the body to a belief in the imperfection of everything else. This is also what I told my students every fall when they sat at their desks, sweaty and mean with the end of a summer, in a school that, though charging each girl an outrageous tuition, scrimped on such basics as air conditioning, decent coffee, and snow days.

Holy Child Academy for Girls was housed on the grounds of a former Vanderbilt estate in Old Brookville. The mansion had twenty-eight rooms, which had been converted into classrooms, lunchrooms, music rooms, art rooms, rooms with ballet bars, and rooms with overstuffed couches, stained glass floor lamps, and faded Turkish rugs donated by aging matrons flown South for the winters of their lives. The grand ballroom was now an acoustically unsound performance hall. A groundskeeper kept the walkways and shrubs lined in seasonal plantings; a riding instructor kept the girls in blue ribbons at the stables; a priest fine-tuned their souls at the chapel. There were six clay tennis courts, two pools (indoor and outdoor), lawns for field hockey, soccer, and lacrosse, and an enormous riding ring. There was an SAT prep coach, a college admissions consultant, and Huckleberry, an English spaniel that wandered the halls, the library, and various offices. A first-rate education for five hundred girls in grades K-12, all for just twenty-five thousand a year. A steal on Long Island's Gold Coast. And on top of that, three security guards to keep them all safe and sound; one manned the front entrance gate from the tiny carriage house, a perfect replica of the big house, another patrolled the grounds in a golf cart, and the other walked the hallways, suspicious of attic noises, groups of girls in bathrooms, pairs of girls walking off into the woods.

What I told them on the first day of school earlier this year: "Sure, you'll get the tools for the SATs. But you're also going to get the equipment for living." I smacked my palm against the blackboard, echoing each word, then wiped it across my pants, smearing a yellow, chalk-dust palm print on my thigh. I don't know why I resorted to such corny gestures, which were met skeptically by all fifteen pairs of sixteen-year-old eyes. They did not believe that I had anything to give them since they had everything money could buy.

Kelsey, third row, fifth from the back, who had been some sort of child actress in Twinkie and Mr. Potato Head commercials, fanned the pages of a notebook back and forth. In the last row, Lara flipped a new haircut back and forth across her shoulders, eyes closed over some summer memory. Mary, daughter of a state senator, admired her manicure. Most either stared at their newly sanitized desks, still gritty with cleanser, or out the windows at the empty lacrosse field and its fresh sod newly striped with white boundary lines, at the banner of yellow mums that spelled out the school initials, HCAG. A few, only a few at this point, looked at me with interest.

Jill Casey had been watching carefully while picking at her peeling, sunburned arms then flicking the bits of skin to the floor. Her older sister, Dawn, had been expelled the previous year for drugs. Dawn played first-string attack for the lacrosse team and when cocaine was found inside her locker, the coach pleaded with the administration to give her another chance since they were on their way to state that year and Dawn would make sure they got there. So they gave her that chance, but then a guard found her and a boy in the boathouse one night, naked, drunk, on some psychedelic, on top of each other, not moving, just passed out. Jill, it was said by the faculty chatting in the rear-parlor-now-lunchroom, was the one who showed real promise: smart, serious, she did not follow in her older sister's footsteps.

I smiled back at Jill, but she had already looked away, chewing on her nails.

So I explained it another way, stepped in front of the windows, threw my arms wide, which worked; their heads tilted in my direction. "What do you need to get through the day? Through a week? A month?"

A few voices offered up food, shelter, clothing, love. "Sex!" yelled Samantha, jangling a stack of silver bracelets like a tambourine.

I laughed along with the class, not to ingratiate myself, but because it was in a way true, but not what I meant. "Okay, yes, I'll give you all that, but don't you need more?"

They hesitated, waited for me to finish. I walked back to the desk, sat on it, sipped coffee then continued, "I thought I knew that what I needed was to be some big shot who drilled holes in brains for a living. But that's because I'd never really thought about it. Obviously since I'm here, I changed my mind. This is what I need."

I leaned back across the desk and removed a notebook from my briefcase. "You'll be keeping a journal. You'll write whatever you want in it as long as you write in it. Hopefully, by the end of the year, you'll have an idea of what you (and here I pointed to a random sampling of girls up and down the rows, finishing with a finger trained on Jill) need to live."

For two months, they had been writing, scribbling, testing out words, waiting for me to read their lives.

I didn't talk to Jill right away. For several days I marked my time, on watch for signs of unhappiness, but she didn't give anything away. She chatted with friends before class about boys and parties, swapped lipstick and gossip. I hadn't read any more of the journal, had buried it, in fact, at the bottom of the box. I was stalling for time, wanting to delay the responsibility of acting or reacting. I didn't want to have to know for a few days longer, didn't want to have to worry about a kid that wasn't mine.

What if I didn't have any words to say? What if there weren't any to help?

Gwen didn't bring it up again, but I could tell she was waiting and watching me for a sign that I had done something, anything except nothing. The box migrated around the apartment, an unspoken accusation. I moved it to the den, Gwen moved it on top of the toilet seat, in front of the door, onto my pillow.

So I tried to fake it. One morning before class started, as Jill sat down at her desk, then rummaged through her backpack for books, I called out to the rest of the class, "Everyone doing okay?" Looked around, listened to the "uh-huhs," called out a few names in particular. "Mary? Samantha? Stephanie? All well with the world? Jill?"

Some smiled back, others looked bored, Jill didn't look up, just fished around at the bottom of her pack for a pen, then lipstick, then a piece of crumpled paper. For the next hour and a half, as I paced back and forth at the front of the room scribbling on the board, reading aloud from _Tess of the D'Urbervilles,_ asking questions: _What does Tess desire? Why does she remain silent for so long? Why must she die in the end?_ I quickly looked down at Jill. Her forehead rested against her hand, eyes hidden by a curtain of brown hair. She hunched over her notebook, diligently underlining passages with her red pen, switching to blue when taking notes. But she was too diligent because I could see that with every passage that we turned to, stopped, and discussed, she underlined every line on the page, trying to shut out everything else except the printed words.

At the end of class, as Jill passed my desk on the way out the door, I asked her if she had liked Hardy, if she was reading other things. She shrugged. "Not really," she said and gathered her books together. She didn't want to talk. Had she lost her faith in me? Did she know I didn't want to ask the right questions? Any questions?

I followed her out into the hall, caught up near the stairs, and tapped her shoulder. Kids pushed past us; a few said, "Hi, Mr. Fitzgerald," which I nodded to, but didn't answer.

"What?" She stood at the top of the stairs, one hand on her hip, the other slid beneath the backpack strapped over her shoulder, and shifted back and forth. "I have another class, you know."

"If you need to talk, I'm all ears...if there's something you need to get off your chest..."

Jill raised her eyebrows at me, looked down and pretended to brush some imaginary object off her breasts. "Nope, nothing there that shouldn't be there."

"I mean, off your mind." Bumbling fumbling Mr. Chips. I didn't know how to say or be what Gwen and Jill wanted me to say or be. I wanted that ultrasound to be wrong, that baby to be a boy, to be someone I could know without feeling foolish and inept.

Jill laughed at me, didn't even try to hide it. "I'm fine, Mr. Fitzgerald. Really. You, on the other hand, are speaking in clichés, and we all know how much you hate the easy way out of language." She patted my shoulder, flashed a wide, blank smile, said, "But thanks for asking," and continued down the stairs, disappearing into the sea of plaid uniforms.

Which is the same thing Gwen had been telling me lately. She was standing in the small second bedroom, not really even in the room, but resting against the door frame. Already the baby's room, my desk, computer, and bookshelves had been moved to the living room months before, replaced with a crib, changing table, and mobile that spun barnyard animals to the tune of "The Farmer in the Dell." But Gwen just stood motionless in the doorway, no sign she'd heard me behind her.

So I asked, "You okay?"

Gwen sighed. "Fine. Just a little tired. Thanks, though, for asking." She'd been up late the past few nights; the baby was kicking right above her bladder and she needed to pee every half-hour. Last night she simply brought a pillow into the bathroom and slept on the floor. "Sometimes it doesn't seem real, like I've just eaten too much and have indigestion. Or severe bloat. Or a bad case of PMS."

I hugged her, trying to touch my fingertips together at the slope of her back, but there were at least five inches of empty space. "No, by my measurements, not PMS. I'd have to agree with Dr. Kessler. Definite baby in there."

She laughed, then sighed into my chest, "I'm afraid."

"The baby's healthy. You're healthy. Everything will be fine."

"What if I'm not healthy? What if my cells harbor some lurking disease or my DNA chain is scrambled? Or I sink into postpartum craziness and want to kill her or myself or turn out to be a shitty, selfish mother and one day she writes that she hates me in big black letters across a journal? And some teacher reads this and doesn't tell me so I never know and I can't change?"

"You drink carrot juice, eat a head of broccoli every day, and brush your teeth with bottled water. You're the poster mother for prenatal perfection. And after she's born, I'll be here to help with the other stuff, and she'll be happy, and we'll be happy."

But Gwen flicked her hand into the air, brushing my words away, and went over to the crib. She swatted at the animals suspended from the mobile; they rattled against each other, strings tangling. "Don't you ever get scared? Don't you ever worry that something might go wrong? What if my body won't let go? What if it freezes and won't give her up?"

I rested my chin on top of her head, which smelled like strawberry shampoo, then kissed it over and over. "No. Because everything has gone right. Everything will be fine. Your body knows what it's doing. The instinct goes back millions of years. We don't even need a doctor. I bet you could squat in the kitchen and on the count of three, I could catch the snap."

She rolled her eyes. "Right. Try passing an eight-pound football through your dick."

"Okay, then, I'll warm the bench and leave it to the pros." I was being corny again, trying to hee-haw away her fears. But what did I really know about being a father? A husband? The Adam to her Eve? And truth be told, I wished that she could spend the next two months in bed, resting, saving her strength, letting me take care of them both.

A week passed without action: I taught *Hamlet*, knew that postponement was fatal. I couldn't sleep, just tossed in bed into the blue hours of night, watching Gwen sleep, her belly rise and fall in time with long, deep breaths. I lusted, ran my hand over her full breasts to her hip and around to her ass. No response, and I wouldn't wake her because she was tired and was only going to get more tired in the coming months; so I tried to help myself, as quiet and still as possible, rolled to one side, and slipped a hand under the sheet.

The downstairs neighbors were fighting—nothing new—about their enormous Rottweiler and how she paid more attention to it than him and how he paid more attention to his dick than her. I kept my hands folded behind my head after that.

Steam banged and clanged through the radiators, hissed on and off. It felt like the eye of a storm was on top of me, waiting for me to move outside. So I got up, went into the kitchen, poured myself a big scotch and read the journal: *I was sitting on the beach alone, at the shoreline, watching the waves creep closer and closer. Jenna and Sarah stayed at the party to find guys to fool around with. In the distance, a sailboat with a light burning inside. All of a sudden, I wanted to swim out to it. I got up and ran into the water. It was cold. I swam maybe fifty feet, it took a while, the waves kept pulling at me. Then I felt something slimy brush against my leg. I'm a baby when it comes to bugs and crabs, so I swam back to shore. I hate myself for not having the courage to keep swimming out and not come back.*

The next morning I stopped in to see the school counselor, Marjorie Williams. On the ride to school, stuck in traffic on the Long Island Expressway, I'd convinced myself that it was the thing to do. Isn't that what Gwen said? Tell someone so something can change?

I had never been in her office but I could see why the kids didn't trust her. Precious Moments figurines lined up along her windowsill, posters of beach sunsets, fields of flowers, clouds and blue sky with accompanying inspirations: "Dare to Dream!" "Be the Best You You Can Be!" "Smile! God Don't Make Junk!" I cringed at the grammar lapse. There were boxes of tissues all over the place, well-positioned props to coax tears. A coffee mug filled with lollipops, the kind with smiling clown faces etched in white sugar. A ratty crocheted blanket bunched in one corner of the worn, green couch; in the other, a giant teddy bear wearing an oversized tee-shirt that read "Need a Hug? I Do!"

Marjorie Williams sat me down on the couch and extended the mug of lollipops. I shook my head so she sat down on her rolling chair and scooted right up to the edge of the couch, inches from my knees. "Well, Mike, what brings you here?" She was nodding and leaning toward me, waiting for me to spill my guts.

"A student."

"Oh," she said, disappointed, as though she'd hoped to hear about trouble at home, a marriage gone bad, a cheating wife, some adult unhappiness. "Who?"

"I don't want to say who. Not yet. I just need some advice. She's in trouble and I wondered what my next step should be."

"Drugs? Sex? Suicide? You should send her down here, you know. That's what I'm here for."

"She seems depressed. I thought I'd talk to her first."

Marjorie crossed her arms across her chest and shook her head, swinging her earrings back and forth. "You don't want to take this on, Mike. You could be held responsible if anything happened and you knew. Just give me her name and I'll get in touch with the parents. That way you can stay out of it and the burden is on me."

"I'm all ready in it."

Marjorie rolled backward to the bookcase, pulled a book from the shelf, and handed over *The Feeling Good Workbook*. She spun to her desk, moved some papers around, then gave me the pamphlet "What To Do When You're Blue," and her business card.

"Give these to her and let her think you're letting her decide. But if she doesn't move on it, then you tell me her name. Trust me, you'll thank me later."

She passed the lollipops again. "And Mike, you know I'm not only here for the kids. If you ever need to talk, just come right on in. Both of you are pregnant, both of you have emotional needs."

Because she was insisting, jangling the mug in front of me, I took a lollipop, felt foolish and fooled.

After dinner one night, Gwen flopped out on the couch, stretched a pair of headphones across her belly, turned on the CD player, and closed her eyes.

I put my ear to her stomach, tried to listen in. It was Gwen's voice, slow, singsong, saying, "It's Mommy. I love you." In the background, Vivaldi's "Four Seasons."

"Gwen," I said, and sat up, "you're losing it."

She opened her eyes, looked suspicious.

I turned the volume all the way up. "Do you really think she can hear this?" Then, rapping my hand gently in the center of her belly, I demanded, "Hellooo in there. What do you think of your crazy mother?"

She slapped my hand and turned the volume back down. "I don't know what she can hear. But if she does, she has to hear so much shit at work with me, has to listen to us, our worries, dumb television shows. If she can hear, I want her to hear good things. There's time enough for the bad."

I leaned back into her belly and whispered, "You are getting very sleepy. You will become a famous composer. You will bring your parents riches beyond their wildest dreams. You will be the first female president, a new messiah, the goddess-on-high herself."

Gwen giggled, pretended to direct an imaginary orchestra across the room, then opened her eyes. "Fine, Mr. Skeptic. If you don't believe in this, then do something useful." She raised a foot and wiggled her toes. "My feet hurt. Get to work."

Later, after the foot massage was over, Gwen cracked open one sleepy eye. "She's humming in here," she whispered, touching her belly, "I swear she's humming an aria. Besides, O most gifted of hands, you can't ever know what she hears inside me. You're stuck on the outside of it all."

I don't think she meant to hurt me, but she did and knew it.

She said quickly, patting my hand, "Look, if it makes you feel any better, I'm on the outside too. Or at least, I will be soon, once she's outside of me."

On Friday afternoon, Jill's class was the last of the day so I asked her to stick around. She waved goodbye to a few friends who said something about a party, then slumped back in her desk and chewed what was left of her nails. I sat next to her, placed her journal on the desk.

"So what's going on?"

She shook her head. "Nothing."

"Don't say that. Don't lie to me."

She looked out the window, at the soccer team lined up in a circle, stretching, twisting, and rolling on their backs. Or maybe at the groups of girls piling into cars, driving off to go shopping, or to shoplift lingerie and condoms, or to someone's house to smoke pot, their parents' pot, or to boyfriends' houses to take showers together, have sex on their parents' beds.

She turned back, looked at me dead-on. "You don't want to know. So just leave me the fuck alone."

"I do know." I tapped my finger on the notebook. "So don't give me that."

"No," she said. "You don't know anything. Nada."

"Are things that bad?"

A hard, quick laugh. "Quite good considering. Dawn's back in rehab, my mom's a bitch, and my dad stays at work late, occasionally comes home, but mostly stays over in the city. Probably having another affair again. And then of course, there's me." She looked away. "But don't even try to figure that one out." She trembled, but not like she was going to cry, more like she wanted to punch me in the face.

I heard myself saying, "Screw your family. You have no reason to hate yourself. You're smart, talented. You have everything going for you." With each word, I felt her close up, fall in and away from me, from my voice, from my stupid patronizing, pacifying words. But I couldn't help it because something else warned me not to get close, to back off; to try and to admit defeat in the same breath.

"What about Mrs. Williams. Could you talk to her?"

She made a face. "Right. I tell her that I hate myself and she calls my parents and then I'll have to listen to them say how I'm just looking for attention, how I have nothing to be depressed about, how they've given me everything that could make me happy. Save it. I heard it all with Dawn."

"Do you want me to talk to your parents?"

She shoved the notebook in her backpack, slung it over her shoulder, and stood up. "Look, Mr. Fitzgerald. I don't expect anything from you. I'm unhappy. No reason, no cure, no hope. I'm a black hole."

"I can't just do nothing."

"You have to. I'm not some after-school special. I don't need you saving me."

I was desperate, fished out *The Feeling Good Workbook* from my briefcase, handed it to her.

She read the name aloud, slowly. "You're kidding. Fill-in-the-blanks and word problems? Gee, you're swell." But she stuffed it in her backpack and left.

As her footsteps echoed down the hallway, I was relieved. She had taken something from me; I had given her something that might, after all, help. For a long while, I sat at the desk watching soccer practice. The girls were strong and fast, sprinting up and down the field, kicking, diving into the grass, using their heads. I knew I fucked up.

This time Gwen was sitting on the floor in the baby's room holding a wallpaper pattern book. We kissed and I touched her belly, imagining the tiny head cupped against my palm. Gwen placed her hands over mine and we rested, welcoming each other, smiling a bit stupidly. There were still these moments that we were completely unprepared for, when suddenly we would grin at each other, giddy and altogether bewildered by what was growing inside of her, at what we had done.

"So," she said, holding the book up, "what do you think?"

The print was busy; ducks, rabbits, dogs, cats, horses, and chickens arranged in repeating order up and down rows across the page. We had been searching Home Depots, specialty stores across the Island, in the city, hundreds of books for a Peter Rabbit print that Gwen had in her childhood bedroom, to no avail.

I shrugged. "It's okay," and handed the book back to her, "but it gives me the creeps. I see chickens and imagine them pecking out each other's eyes. I saw that once, at a petting zoo when I was a kid. I just don't want to have to think about that every time I come in here at night to feed the baby. It's unhealthy."

Gwen raised the book over her head and hurled it at the wall. It left a black mark in the white, chalky paint. "This is ridiculous!" she shouted. "Why is wallpaper so impossible for us? Are we that incapable already?"

"Look," I said, "prenatal psychology isn't working. We'll never know, really, what this baby will want or whether mutilated chickens will be the stuff of nightmares. So I think we need to just put that aside and make a decision and not worry so much about it."

"No," she said, glaring and shaking her head back and forth, "it has to be perfect. Nature, nurture, environment— it's everything." And then she turned on me. "What about that girl? Jill Casey? Have you done anything to help her?"

"I tried to talk to her. I gave her this book on depression."

"So you don't have to worry so much about it? Mike, honey, you have to worry about it. That's the point. You are responsible for the worrying. Nobody in her family wants to. So you're It."

And a lousy It at that.

On Sunday, we went to my mother-in-law's for dinner. Jean lived out in Riverhead at Forest Glen, an expensive retirement community. I hated going there; it seemed unnatural, antiseptic. All of the houses were one story with a non-optional wheelchair ramp leading up to the front door, and the only kids around were grandkids who couldn't visit for longer than a week at a time or use the swimming pool between the hours of 9 A.M. and 4 P.M.

Jean wasn't even that old, had actually lied about her age to get in. The minimum requirement was sixty-eight, she was sixty-five. I didn't think I would feel comfortable bringing the baby here, a baby who might cry too loudly, disturb the expensive peace, demand too much.

We were sitting on the couch after a dinner of pot roast and potatoes, paging through old albums. Jean clung to all memorabilia with fierce determination, told Gwen she'd get all her old things when she was dead and buried. But only then. She didn't want people pawing through her stuff while she was still alive. "Besides," she told her when Gwen first tried to pack up her collection of Little Golden Books to take to our apartment, "that way you'll want to come back. I'll still have a few bits and pieces of you." Gwen didn't begrudge her mother this stubborn quirk; her husband was dead, her only child married, most of her friends had long since moved to Coral Gables, and I had recently buried her senile Chihuahua in the flower bed out back beneath a cluster of marigolds. The leftovers of others, the only things that remained, were the only things that still needed daily tending.

A black and white photo fell out from a yellowed page: Gwen sitting on the top step leading into Our Lady of Sorrows School in Ridgewood, plaid kilt hemmed just below her knees, hair drawn back into a ponytail trimmed with a white ribbon. At thirteen her legs and arms are long and skinny, poke out from the cuffs like awkward afterthoughts. She is smiling wide but looking past the lens to the photographer in cool suspicion. Between her legs, a flash of white underwear cuts into her thighs; she is unaware or perhaps too aware of what has been revealed.

I wanted to punch the pervert who snapped the photo, who coaxed young schoolgirls into letting down their guard, into trusting him. "Look," I pointed. My finger covering the flash of white.

Gwen took the photo, held it close up, then at an arm's length away, covered one eye, then the other. "You have to be looking pretty hard there to see that. Besides, Mom took the picture. And however many problems we may have had at the time, I don't think she was into kiddie porn."

"What problems?" Her mother leaned over to get a better look at the picture. "We didn't have any problems. Look at you, you look beautiful there. But Mike's right. How could I not have noticed that? Mothers are supposed to keep an eye out for frayed hems, untucked shirts, clean underwear. All those small details."

Gwen frowned at the photo, rubbing her thumb across the body of the girl on the stairs. I didn't want to tell her that the oils from her finger could cause deterioration, because she was reading the flat surface as if it contained a secret message in braille. She slipped the picture back beneath the loose, plastic cover, laughed sharply. "You didn't notice a lot of things, Mom, like when I ate a whole bottle of aspirin."

Her mother stiffened. "I noticed that you were a happy girl. That nonsense was an accident. Why do you have to bring that up anyway? What is Mike going to think?" She strode into the kitchen, smacking open cupboards, banging mugs down on the table.

"What do you think, Mike?" Gwen asked.

I had never heard about the aspirin and waited for Gwen to say more, but her eyes were closed and she smoothed a palm back and forth over her belly. I stopped her, placed my hand over hers.

She opened her eyes and said, "That was a long time ago. I was stupid and young. For an entire day I was puking and sweating and had ringing in my ears before I told my parents anything. At the hospital, my mother and father maintained that I had a bad headache and was desperate for relief." She took a deep breath, hugged her arms around her belly. "But I don't want to talk about it. She might hear."

Her mother came back in the room, handed out the coffee and tea, smiled brightly. "I have an idea. Let's look at slides. It's been years since we did that."

I scavenged around in the garage until I found the screen and projector, Gwen searched the back storage room for the boxes of slides, and her mother shouted to both of us that what we were looking for was in this corner or that, behind the box of ornaments, behind the winter coats. It took an hour to assemble the screen, put slides in the carrel, close the shades, and whip cream for the shortcake.

Her mother had chosen slides from a box labeled "Cape Cod, 1965," and provided the running commentary: "That was on Nauset Beach... your first trip to the beach, let's see, you must have been four months. *Click.* And see your Dad, Mr. Don Ho himself, trying to body surf. He was all cut up from the shells and rocks by the time he was through. *Click.* That's me, changing your diaper, trying to keep the sand out of it. *Click.* That's our first lobster dinner and that's you crying and crying and the restaurant asked us to leave so your dad took his lobster and threw it at the manager. *Click.* Look how little you were, in your pink suncap and Mickey Mouse bib. How could anyone complain? *Click.* There's the three of us, your father's first attempt with the self-timer. Look how happy we are."

Gwen tottered up from the couch and stood beside the stream of hot light. On the screen, the silhouetted profile of her belly covered her father. Waving at the camera, he stood behind her mother who smiled beneath a large straw hat, holding Gwen who was asleep, dreaming to the sound of the waves.

Her mother sat up straight, patted Gwen away, and clicked to the next picture: Gwen, wide-eyed and naked, hands reaching up and out to her father, her mother, the clouds. "Just you two wait. You think babies are all cute and cuddly now, but wait until she has diarrhea or colic and cries all night. Wait until she spikes a fever and you think she's going to die and all you can do is wait it out. Just wait and hope your baby doesn't die."

Gwen cupped her hands around the stream of light. They pushed the light back, finally resting across the hot bulb on the projector. The room went dark. "Enough, Mom. We've seen enough."

Later, driving back to our apartment, Gwen took my right hand from the steering wheel and pressed the photograph into it. I glanced down as we passed beneath a street lamp. The young smiling Gwen flashed in my palm, a bright white splotch against the black background, then passed into darkness, then flashed bright again under the next lamp, then darkness. I dropped it between us on the seat waiting for her to explain the theft. She had never taken anything from her mother, at least nothing concrete.

She turned to the window, forehead pressed against it. "On the surface I was all smiles. But sitting in the back row of class, I was terrified no one would notice my loneliness. And at the same time, terrified that someone would. So please, Mike, for me, do something. The right something."

I reached across the seat for her hand but couldn't find it because it was covering her face. We'd been married for four years, but there was much that I didn't know about my wife.

When we went to bed that night, I inched my way slowly to her across our too big bed, touching first her ear, then neck, kissing her eyelids, pressing my hand against her belly. But she shrugged me off.

"I don't feel like talking."

"I wasn't talking. I was touching you."

"But you want to talk. I can feel it." She ran her hand over her belly and sighed. "Just let tonight be. Okay?"

In the morning, Gwen's sadness was gone, secreted safely away from me, from our happiness.

Monday morning I tacked the photograph of Gwen to the corkboard above my desk in the office, beside a more recent photo of her at Jones Beach—tanned, smiling, her stomach half the size it was now—and on top of brochures Marjorie Williams stuck in my mailbox: "Considerations for Students from Broken Homes," "How to Welcome and Watch a Student from Rehab," "10 Signs a Teen Is Suicidal," "Date Rape 101."

I dug around my desk for *The Feeling Good Workbook* (Marjorie sent me an extra copy, Post-it note attached: *Just in case you might need one...*), and opened to lesson one: "Optimism is a habit. On the lines below, take inventory of your assets. Write down twenty things from your life's ledger that contribute to your net worth. It is impossible to expect more from the Universe when you don't appreciate the things you already have."

No wonder Jill hated Marjorie Williams. If she had opened the book over the weekend, if she had sat down on her bed in her empty house listening to the empty echo inside her, what could she have written? She would have seen through the ploy, would have turned its optimism on its head. What would she have written? *Assets: My mother, when she's not a bitch. My father, when he's at home and fucking my mother, not his girlfriend. Dawn, when she's not strung out. Me, when I don't hate me.*

I didn't know what I would do, maybe not the right thing, because what was that? But I would do something.

In class that day, Jill refused to look at me, no matter how much I flailed my arms and paced back and forth. It was poetry week, and I was reciting parts of "Song of Myself" from memory, was looking out at the girls, watching their faces for a response, trying to send Jill a signal through Whitman: *Long have you timidly waded, holding a plank by the shore,/ Now I will you to be a bold swimmer,/ To jump off in the midst of the sea, and rise again and nod to me and shout,/ and laughingly dash with your hair.*

In front of her desk, I paused, glanced down, hoping to see her nod in understanding, but saw instead jagged lines extending beyond the cuffs of her white uniform blouse. Not lines, but scabbed-over slashes.

I caught my breath.

How did I get through the next forty minutes of class? I don't remember. All I can remember is trying not to look at her, trying to hold on to Whitman's words, trying not to get sick.

I kept her after class and, against protocol, closed the classroom door. Steady, I told myself, steady. Deep breath.

"What did you do to yourself?"

"What do you mean," she said, clenching the cuffs to her palms.

"I saw what you did. I saw it," I said, angry now, and grabbed her hand. I knew all the lawsuits: I knew what could happen when a male teacher touches a female student, but I didn't care, just held on to her and pushed back her sleeve.

She winced, "You're hurting me. Let go." She pulled away but I tightened my grip.

"Let go of me," she yelled, "you don't know anything." Then she kicked me hard in the shin.

"Stop it," I said, "stop it." I wanted to shake her, slap her quiet, but restrained myself. I jerked back one sleeve and saw the gashes—deep, open mouths pulled tight across the thin skin of her wrists—then let her go. I knew enough.

I struggled for something to say that could hide my horror. Not at what she'd done, but at what I hadn't done. "How could you do this to yourself?"

She shrugged. "There was nothing else to do."

"I can't handle this," I said. "Legally, professionally. I can't, not by myself."

She turned back to me, her eyes wide, pleading. "No. You can't tell anyone. My parents will kill me."

"Jill, they won't kill you. They need to know." True, but not the truth: I needed them to know.

"They don't. You don't know them." She was shaking her head, her fists balled tight to her sides. "I hate you."

"I can live with that," I said. She was someone's daughter and all I could think about was how alone she was, how she needed someone to watch out for her, someone other than me who didn't know the words that could save anyone.

Marjorie wheeled over to Jill and handed her the teddy bear. Jill hurled it across the room, crossed her arms over her chest, and glared at us.

Marjorie rolled closer to me. "Mike," she said, hand touching my shoulder, "you did the right thing."

"I don't know," I said. And I didn't any longer. Jill had even less than before and I should have tried harder, stuck it out a little longer, not given in to my chickenshit and Marjorie's bullshit.

Marjorie rolled to her desk, picked up the phone, and called Jill's house. Someone answered and Marjorie whispered into the receiver, nodded her head, and soothed, "She's okay. She's here. We'll be here."

"Well," she said, after hanging up, "that was your Mom." She rolled back over to Jill, leaned forward, head in hands, elbows on knees, the perfect studied pose of concern. "Do you want me to tell you what she said?"

Jill didn't answer.

"I will anyway. She's very upset. Not with you, but with this situation. She's very worried, sweetheart. We all are." Marjorie nodded at me. "She had no idea, Mike." Then she nodded at Jill. "She's calling your dad at work to meet you at the hospital."

Jill looked us carefully over. "Thank you," she said. "Thank you both for ruining my life."

I waited with them until her mother arrived. For a half hour, Jill was silent, fell away from us, the room, the hysteria around her, into her emptiness. Marjorie chattered on and on about how things would get better for her, how she was going to get the help she needed, how her parents were going to help her. I wanted to throttle Marjorie, at the very least, report her to a state agency for incompetent platitudes.

But wasn't that all I had done? She was a counselor, trained to deal with disruptive classroom behaviors, with learning difficulties, with providing information about mental health resources. Real emergencies were handled off school grounds for $300 an hour in dark, anonymous, mahogany-paneled offices. She was a clearinghouse, not a psychologist, not a psychiatrist, but a counselor and not a very good one. She knew that, though, didn't she? Wasn't that what all the props were for?

Except now she was talking quietly to Jill, stroking her arm, careful to keep her fingertips on top of her forearms, and Jill, nodding and shaking her head, was listening. And then, to my surprise, Jill turned her arms over, palms up, unbuttoned the cuffs and pushed back the white sleeves all the way to her elbows, and showed Marjorie what she had done. The awful, terrible, lonely damage.

Marjorie swallowed hard, then held both of Jill's hands, looked at her directly in the eyes, and said, "It's okay, sweetheart. It's okay. You won't have to do this again. Okay? I can see how bad it is. You've shown me and I know." And then Marjorie inched the sleeves back down, one at a time, careful of the cuffs skimming over the wounds, then buttoned them closed at her wrists.

And then Jill's mother rushed in, blonde hair piled high on top of her head, makeup slapped on in a hurry. Slash of eyeliner, messy swatch of lipstick, streak of rouge, keys clutched tight in her hand. She threw herself at Jill, begged to know what she had done, why she didn't tell her, but Jill stayed silent.

Her mother looked to Marjorie, to me, "How?" she said, her eyes wide, hand grasping her throat, trying to stem the panic.

Jill plucked at loose threads on the couch cushion, wound one long, green thread tight around her finger, stopping her blood.

"Please," her mother begged, after a few silent moments, "can I see?"

Jill yanked her finger free and clamped them together as if in desperate prayer.

Her mother ran her fingers over Jill's hands, tried to pull them apart, but they wouldn't budge. "Please, Jilly, it's Mommy."

Jill shook her head, trying not to give in, trying to hold herself away from us all, from the people who had failed her.

I felt terrible for Jill, but maybe more for her mother. She was stunned, helpless in the face of a daughter she didn't know, a daughter who didn't want her to know. And she was being told all about it by two strangers who knew more about her daughter than she did. It was time for me to leave. I stood, gathered my briefcase and jacket, said to Jill, "I'm sorry," nodded to her mother, and left.

Marjorie knew, too, and followed. "Really, Mike," she said, "this is too big for either of us to fix by ourselves."

That night in bed, Gwen listened as I rubbed cream into the stretch marks that fissured out from her bellybutton across her tight, watery skin. She was worried she'd be stuck with them forever and was trying to counteract the damage. Her belly seemed enormous, as if it had doubled in density from the morning. I wondered how it felt to have the weight of a child pulling at her insides, six or seven pounds of gravity pulling on her ribs, lungs, heart.

I pressed my nose into her bellybutton, imagining the baby's nose against mine, separated only by the thin wall of tissue. "How could they not know?" I whispered to her.

"Not know what?" Gwen said.

"How could they live in the same house as their daughter and not know? Not sense that something was wrong?"

Gwen sighed and ruffled her hands through my hair. "Easy. Just because she's yours doesn't mean you want to know."

"I'll want to know," I said, and patted her belly, hoped ours could hear me.

"You won't," Gwen said. "Because once you know, you can never be sure of her happiness again. Or your own."

Was Jill home by now? Did a doctor at the hospital take care of her, was he able to explain things to her parents, tell them what to do to help their daughter? Was she asleep now, buried under the covers? Were her parents huddled at the kitchen table, trying to pinpoint where they had gone wrong, when they had missed the signs? Would they sneak into her bedroom in the deep hours of night, penlight in hand, lift the covers from their sleeping daughter, push back the sleeves of her nightgown, and shine the small circle of light on her wrists, searching for an explanation? Absolution? Would they ever get a good night's sleep again? Or would they wake up at the slightest noise, a creak, a toilet flushing, water running in the bathroom sink, and wonder if it was Jill, if she was okay, why she was up alone in the dark, if she was sitting on the toilet, razor to wrist?

But soon I would know. Soon I would hold my own daughter, wonder at her small scalloped fingernails, the soft concave spot on her skull. Soon she would pull herself to a crawl, then a few tentative steps, a few words. And then I would hold her in my lap and read her fairytales, the smoothed-over versions, not the blood and gristle of the Brothers Grimm, not the fathers and mothers who eat their children. She would get Walt Disney, the benign Technicolor of *The Little Mermaid*. So what if the grit was lost in the rated-G translation? So what if the little mermaid no longer felt knives pushing into her feet where fins once grew? Wasn't it better this way, the mermaid safe and sound, happy ever after, ad infinitum? No, I couldn't ever relax because I would miss something. In a moment, she could swim away and I could lose her in that ocean.

THE BODY/LOVE PROBLEM

For many years, I lived without desire, never considered it, made no provisions for it in a body that was loyal, quiet, logical. I was fast approaching middle age, with a daughter in college and a husband who loved me in fact, if not in passionate practice. When making love, tranquil love now, we closed our eyes against the memory of our beginnings and tried to remake real love, conjure it up from the safety of our contentment failed. In suburban terms, we were a successful couple: David an orthopedic surgeon; I, a piano teacher; our twenty-five-year marriage assured of longevity, already outlasting many of our friends. We still genuinely liked each other, could make each other laugh, went out on dinner dates and movie dates alone, without other couples to furnish conversation, still had more in common than an intelligent and athletic daughter who played lacrosse at Georgetown.

I thought it was enough, that I was beyond moony feelings and quick burn, that I could satisfy those occasional urges on my own. It's not that David and I didn't make love, we did, regularly every week or so, but making love was comfortable, safe, pleasant, like a good back rub. There was no urgency, just a lovely sigh when we came together, a quick kiss on the forehead, and we rolled over to sleep, dreaming our own separate, vague dreams. We would rise the next morning into our happiness like the dead into eternity: sure that since we had crossed over with each other, there was nothing that we could lose any longer, nothing else we could ever need.

I taught piano from home. David had converted half of our two-car garage into a studio years earlier. And though we had the money to hire contractors, he insisted on building it himself and devoted his days off to erecting drywall, painting, installing baseboard heaters, soft green carpet, and bright track lighting that gleamed off the black baby grand he buffed to a shine each week. "It's a labor of love, Helena," he said, when I suggested professionals might be faster, save him his days off. When the studio was finally finished, he pulled me down to the floor, waggled his eyebrows, nipped at my breasts, and in his best rakish voice, said "Now let's labor at love, baby." We laughed and gave ourselves easily, entirely to each other, trusting our bodies to follow their natural inclinations. For two years, every Sunday, after my regular three-hour practice (and it was practice; by the end I was sweaty, exhausted, fingers aching and cramping into claws), we made love on that carpet. For two years we each had a matching pair of faint red circles on our shoulder blades, rug burns, marks of our desire. And then one Sunday, we forgot, then I was tired, then he had a cold, and finally the big, soft, king-sized bed upstairs seemed more comfortable for lovemaking and one step closer to sleep.

Every afternoon, a steady stream of students came for their lesson, most of them sullen and pissed off that they had to give up time with friends for an hour tied to a bench. Who could blame them? Their mothers saw tiny prodigies, imagined little Beethoven, Schubert, and Rachmaninoff homunculi dazzling relatives at family reunions, wowing the President, First Lady, and various heads of state at the White House, then all of Hollywood at the Oscars, bragging rights to a true family genius. Of course, most of the kids were terrible—not because they were naturally inept (though some were certainly better suited for the full-body contact of drums than the graceful athletics of piano), but because they wouldn't practice.

I was relatively famous in our town since I was an actual graduate of Julliard and had played Carnegie Hall several times many years ago before marrying David, thus was considered a bona fide professional rather than some high school music teacher looking to make a few bucks on the side. I willingly traded a career as a musician for David, his love, safety, and tenderness without regret. At heart, I was decidedly suburban, afraid to live the uncertain life of a free agent, ricocheting between orchestras, lonely cities, and short-term gigs. What I really wanted was not fame, adventure, or independence, but someone who loved me, who I could love. And what I really knew was that I was ultimately a practical pianist, not a virtuoso, that I was terrified of being found out, had been running myself into the ground trying to prove I was something more than what I was: a good accompanist.

David had stumbled into a practice session one January evening looking for his girlfriend, a willowy flutist who had two nervous breakdowns in as many years, and wound up sitting in the back row for two hours, listening to my practicing, screwing up, cursing, and finally perfecting for one single run through Beethoven's First Concerto. When I finally pushed in the bench, he walked over and took my tired, cold hands in his gloved ones and said, "That was beautiful. Wonderfully, absolutely beautiful." I shivered, not from the cold but from the way he was looking at me. "Here," he said, tugging off his gloves, "put these on." His hands were larger than mine and an inch of green wool flopped over each fingertip but I stretched my fingers into the warmth his hands had left behind.

Then the flutist stomped in, her pale blond hair gathered in a meticulous chignon, a red diaphanous scarf draped around her neck, its ends billowing down her back like flames, heels clacking across the floor. She glared at him, then briefly at me. What did she see? Long brown hair clipped back in a ponytail, bare face, nose red and runny, gloved hands, pilly pink sweater long overdue for the garbage. She sniffed, dismissing my importance, and demanded an explanation: why hadn't he been where he said he'd be? She'd been waiting outside for the past hour, shivering and pacing the block, afraid he was dead. David shrugged and said, "I got sidetracked. I'm sorry." They left, but he came back a week later. "For the gloves?" I asked, and pulled them out of my purse. "For you," he said. And that was that.

I taught Ethan's daughter, Rebecca, first. She was ten, had been taking lessons for two years and actually wanted to; she didn't fidget or forget to practice her scales, but rushed into the studio each week, blond hair tied up in a ponytail that switched across her shoulders with impatience, notebook clasped to her chest, hands itching to leap, arch, and tumble across the keys.

Ethan, her father, came second. Dede his wife, and my occasional tennis partner at the country club, had given him a year's worth of piano lessons for his forty-ninth birthday. "It'll keep Ethan busy," she said. "A mid-life crisis is looming on the horizon, and I'd rather he take up something constructive, something other than a Harley and younger women."

I knew enough not to be insulted. In the past year alone, three husbands and two wives from the club got new haircuts, lost weight, started drinking exotic martinis at bars in the city, and then left their spouses for something less constructive, more destructive and enticing than round-robin tennis tournaments, sedate New Year's Eve dinner dances, lasagna buffets, and pot-luck barbecues. Last summer, when the first husband left, then the first wife, then the second and third, we lounged around the pool in our chaises under the shade of green-striped umbrellas watching the abandoned spouses herd the abandoned children to the snack bar for hamburgers and frozen Snickers bars, then wander morosely to the real bar for gin and tonics at noon. We pitied them, clucked with them over their horror stories in consolation, offered shoulders to cry on, but didn't get too close, afraid that their bad luck would rub off on us as we sunned ourselves in the warm felicity of our marriages.

We decided on Wednesday evenings. Ethan didn't want to come on the same day as his daughter because he didn't want to make her self-conscious or think he was trying to best her. "Believe me," he said, "she's the one with talent. I can barely get my shirt buttoned on straight without Dede. Besides, this is her crazy idea. She said that the right side of my brain was beginning to bulge out like a tumor and the left side shriveling up like a prune. She wants me to try to exercise my creative muscles." His voice trailed off. Ethan, though working in advertising, was a vice president on the business end; he put deals together, made sure campaigns increased profits, didn't actually come up with the witty slogans or strategies.

"You won't actually bench-press the piano, you know. You'll play it."

He laughed, more at ease.

I was trying to dispel the embarrassment I heard in his voice, the nervousness I'd never heard in him before. But then, we'd never really talked on the phone before. Of course, he answered the phone when I called his home, but then immediately passed me off to his wife. That was how it was here: wives arranged mixed doubles and dinner dates with other wives, not other husbands. So it felt strange talking to Ethan like this, more like arranging an indiscretion than a business appointment. Dede should be setting up the schedule, keeping tabs, marking territory.

"Oh, I wouldn't go so far as to say I'll be playing it, making noise is more like it," he said. "I'm afraid I'm bound to disappoint Dede whatever I manage to do."

"Look, whatever happens during the lessons is between us. If you're tone deaf, an absolute horror, I won't be the one to blow the whistle on you. Think of me as a shrink: I cannot be compelled to testify against you."

"Unless my playing puts lives in jeopardy and starts to kill off the hearing population," he said.

"Don't worry," I said. "All you need is the desire to play and the willingness to practice. And I won't force you to play after Rebecca in the spring recital."

"Thank you, Helena," he said, "and now since you're my musical shrink, I'll tell you a secret."

"Okay." I smiled. It was not often that a man other than my husband told me his secrets.

He took a deep breath. "I've actually always dreamed of playing the piano, of being able to come home after a long day of work, and with a scotch in hand, play, if not Beethoven, then Billy Joel into the blue hours of the night."

He hung up before I could say a word, though I'm not sure what I would have said. Not many men would say things like that to their daughter's teacher, their wife's friend, to someone who had seen him flopping a backstroke in the country club pool in plaid swim trunks, to someone who could laugh at his foolish whimsy. He'd violated the rules, let loose a desire, a secret. What was I supposed to do with it? Return the serve in kind? I didn't believe that I had any long-buried desires, at least, none that I would tell to a man who wasn't my husband. None that I would tell to anyone at all.

First lesson: he rushed in straight from work, pin-striped suit and shiny black shoes. It was unexpected, he looked handsome, unlike himself, not like Dede's husband. I was used to seeing him in khakis, polo shirts, Top-Siders. I glanced down at my jeans, plain black tee shirt, and tennis sneakers and felt my age and under dressed, wanted to hide my forty-six-year-old body that yielded contentedly to gravity's tug. I knew I looked exactly the same to him. The playing field needed to be leveled, made safe and familiar, so I told him he might be more comfortable without his jacket and tie, and blushed as if I'd asked him to remove more. I thumbed through a book of scales, averting my eyes trying to regain control—nothing had changed except we were now dealing with each other alone, unhinged from our spouses.

He took off his jacket, but only loosened his tie and unbuttoned the top button on his shirt. Then he waved the tie at me. "It's one of those Jerry Garcia ties. The Grateful Dead guy. Dede bought it for me yesterday, figured it might get me into a more creative mind-set."

It didn't seem especially psychedelically inspired, just blotches of brown and yellow and purple thrown onto silk.

"Ugly isn't it? Like vomit," he said. "I can't picture any deadheads wearing them. Just a bunch of graying ad execs looking to keep up with the younger crowd." He let go of the tie and it flopped back on his chest. "But, it makes Dede happy so I'll wear it."

"What we do for love," I said, and we laughed. "David bought me this hideous shirt, you know, puffy sleeves, shoulders like Cinderella? I wore it once then accidentally scorched it with an iron."

"So a big blob of well-placed ketchup might ruin the tie?"

"Ketchup would blend in. But grease?"

He wagged his finger. "This is a side of you I've never seen."

"It's better than having to lie about it being lost day in and day out when you know it's crammed into the back of a drawer. You loved it but now it's ruined."

"So rather than tell him he doesn't know what you like..."

"Exactly. Feelings spared." I dragged my chair next to the piano and pulled out the bench for him.

He shrugged. "Now what?"

"Now we play. But first I need to see your wrists."

"Helena, I'm not that nervous. My playing might kill others, but I'm not about to kill myself over it," he said, turning up his palms to me.

I hesitated, then leaning over, pushed his shirt cuffs back and turned his hands back over, resting them on top of the keys. "I need to see your wrists in order to watch your form." A phrase I repeated again and again to my students only now, with Ethan, it sounded like an innuendo.

It was strange being alone together, without the safety of David and Dede. I had never imagined Ethan without Dede, and he had probably never imagined me without David. The suburbs solidify coupledom: we travel in pairs to movies and dinners and dances, have same-sex friends, are never alone with each other's husbands or wives. Safety in numbers. Everybody already claimed.

For an hour, I pulled Ethan's fingers into position and he learned a few basic scales with fingers tripping over each other.

"Shit," he grumbled, trying to stretch his hands across the keys. He clenched his jaw and for several seconds stared down at his hands, flexing them, curling them up. Then he balled his right hand into his left and cracked his knuckles, one after another. "I'm not cut out for this, Helena," he said, and banged his fists down on the keys, a bit harder than he intended. He jumped back at the jangle of sound and pulled his hands back.

"Ethan, it's okay, really. You can't hurt it unless you can pick it up and toss it out the window. Otherwise, go ahead and bang away if that's what you feel like doing. I do it myself. I'm frustrated? I pound away." I took his hands in mine; they stiffened at my touch, but then relaxed. I led them back to the keys and placed my hands on top of his, to guide them through a few scales like I often did with my beginning students. But I was used to the smooth tiny hands of children, the long and delicate hands of teenage girls, or David's soft, immaculate fingers. Not these bulky hands covered in tiny curls of dark hair. I couldn't find my balance, couldn't decide how to be because his hands felt strange and different beneath mine. And I felt different and strange, very much in my body, instead of out of it, which is how I usually felt during lessons—all ears. And suddenly my stomach felt flabby, breasts saggy, breath stale, then the stubble on my calves itched, then the stubble on my thighs itched, then the stubble along my bikini line itched and itched and itched, which I tried to nonchalantly scratch with my forearm, then elbow. I was miserable, wanted out of my body.

At the end of the hour, he grinned, just like his daughter, and said, "Helena, you're a genius." I don't know why he said that since I didn't really do anything, and all he'd played was "Twinkle Twinkle Little Star," but I also knew that I was beginning to fill up his empty ache, his desire finally met, and felt guilty. After he left, I did fifty quick sit-ups, took a shower, shaved my legs with a new razor, gargled mouthwash, and rubbed raspberry cream into my skin until I was sticky, disgusted with myself, the lack of attention to detail, the body that had fallen apart.

And yet, behind all of this primping, was something more: we'd swapped secrets. Mine? Ridiculous, indicating only a one-time dissatisfaction with David's gift. Okay, more than a one-time dissatisfaction. And maybe I expected that after all those years of marriage he might have a better idea about my taste in clothes. Hardly anything indicating global dissatisfaction, though it was something I wouldn't tell David and something I had told Ethan.

Things continued like this for several weeks. I found myself exchanging baggy jeans for long silky skirts and my younger students started asking if I was going out someplace special that night. I didn't want to directly connect my new attention to detail to Ethan until David brought it up one night. He was stretched out on the couch in the studio, thumbing quickly through a medical journal. I was practicing Bach's Fantasia in C Minor, lousing it up.

"So, Helena, do I have to worry about competition from some budding teenage genius?"

I didn't have any pimply seventeen-year olds, only Ethan with his receding hairline and clumsy hands.

I stopped, my hands faltering. "What do you mean?"

"Don't 'what do you mean?' me. You know what I mean. You've traded in sweats for silk, new haircut, and you don't smell like you. You smell like fruit. Exotic, South Seas Island fruit."

I could feel his eyes on my back waiting for an answer, but I was angry at his implication. "You know David, not everything I do is for other people. Some things are only for me." I twisted around to face him and thumped on my chest. "Me. I look in the mirror and see someone who has gotten very sloppy, very lazy. I might as well have been wearing a housedress and slippers. I forgot I inhabited the body of a living, breathing woman. That's all. So I decided to try to pull myself together. For me."

David sank back into the couch and gave a great exaggerated sigh. "Well, I'll be damned, folks. Here's one for the medical journals. My wife's a woman: breasts, vagina, heart and all."

I turned back to the piano and began playing again, striking the keys as hard as I could.

Then his hands were on my shoulders, fingers pressing down into the bones, his chin resting on top of my head. "I'm glad you're doing it for you. Really. But I had hoped that part of you was doing it for me, too."

I held his hands to my shoulders, covered them with mine. "All you doctors are egomaniacs."

His soft fingers slid my dress off one shoulder, lips followed. He made love to me that night on the floor of the studio, something we hadn't done in years, and I wrapped my legs all the way around his back like when we practiced Tantric sex in the seventies, only my feet couldn't flatten together like they used to. He pushed deep inside me as if he was trying to break through, to discover whatever it was I was being secretive about. I locked my thighs against him, holding him close to my body, and tried to moan, encouraging him on, hoping I sounded there, with him, an active and passionate participant. But it didn't come out right, sounded more like a whimper.

He pulled out. "Did I hurt you?"

I shook my head. Nothing I couldn't stand.

He touched my eyes, tapped lightly against the closed lids. "Look at me. Helena."

My eyes had been closed tight the entire time, shut against his solid body outlined by the dim shadows of light and I didn't even notice. But David did. I opened them. David was hovering over me, arms locked as if doing push-ups, long, taut veins drawn out on his forearms. He frowned and rolled off onto his back, then said, "Where the hell are you, Helena?" He was staring up at the ceiling, hands folded on top of his chest.

I crouched on top of him, slid my hand across his stomach, then further, coaxing him back. "Here," I said. "I'm here, on top of you, making love to you. I thought you were also making love to me."

"I thought we were making love," he said.

"Just shut up, David. You're ruining the moment with talk." I pushed his hands back over his head and lowered myself against him; he didn't seem to object.

We were at the club one hot August afternoon and had arranged a doubles match with Dede and Ethan. We decided to swap partners, David and Dede against Ethan and me. It was only fair since Dede and Ethan were serious players, in winter leagues and weeknight games, while David and I were weekenders, content to play a set or two then plop down at the bar for a beer, a wine spritzer, and goldfish crackers. But suddenly, on opposing sides, we took to the game with new ferocity. For the first set, David's backhand was dead-on down the line, my serve accurate with top spin; we both basked in the approval of our partners.

Every time we switched sides, Ethan would rest his hand on my shoulder as we walked around the net, and say, "We can do it, Helena. Just keep it up and stay focused." Dede and David walked around the opposite end of the net silently, without comment.

By the end of the first set, which they won 7-5, Dede's face was tight and red, David's still and empty. In the second set, Dede made careless mistakes, lobbing balls against the back fence, serving them far beyond the base line. David's backhand dissipated and he loped to the net, shrugged when he missed easy shots. I took advantage of his fluff balls, Dede's miscalculations, and spun returns into the distant corners of the court, at Dede's feet, to David's backhand. Every time I hit a winner, I looked at Ethan, who smiled and clapped his hand against his racket. I felt strong, mean, and determined. No longer the pussy-foot piano teacher, but the more feminine reincarnation of Billie Jean King.

We could have won six-love, but somehow, through unspoken agreement, Ethan and I pulled back and let them have two games. We realized we were being careless, losing control, taking unfair advantage of our new intimacy: we were no longer bound by the same rules of propriety as our spouses since, after all, once a week for the past two months we'd been brushing shoulders and knees, seemingly talking about music.

We sat under the courtside canopy for a break, watched the games in progress on other courts.

"A tie-breaker set?" Ethan asked.

Dede dabbed her forehead with a wristbanded wrist and nodded at David, then me. "I'd love to, but Ethan promised Rebecca he'd take her golfing this afternoon." She glanced at her watch. "It's up to you, Ethan, but you said one o'clock." Dede turned to me and shrugged. "He doesn't get much quality time with Rebecca. Eighteen holes reserves a big chunk of quantity time."

David sighed. "Hell, hon, I'm pooped. I could use a swim. Or a drink. Both." He stretched back in his chair and draped his arm carefully around my shoulder; it felt prickly and hot and I wanted to shrug it off but let it stay. You love this man, I told myself, but I was looking at Ethan who was looking at me, and I could feel Dede's eyes moving from Ethan, to me, forming an oblique accusation.

So I jumped up, ran my fingers underneath the elastic of my tennis panties, which were cutting into my skin. "A swim sounds good. It'll take the edge off the heat."

Dede waded around in the shallow end and bobbed up and down, keeping her hair and made-up face above the water line. David, after a quick dunk, plopped down in a chaise and snoozed in the sun. Ethan swam laps. I hugged the side wall at the deep end, fluttering my legs through the water, and tilted my face to the sky, to the waves of light, listening to the clatter of voices at the snack bar. And then I felt a hand on my foot, was startled, jerked out of my meditation, and looked down into the clear, blue, over-chlorinated water.

Ethan hovered several feet down, hair swimming away from his scalp, smiling and blowing bubbles up to me. He held on to my ankle with one hand, the other slid up my smooth calf, to my thigh. I felt like I was underwater, unable to breathe, just sinking slowly to the bottom, to the drain. I knew I should swim away, that it would be an embarrassing, awful scene if Dede or David or anyone else happened to look down at us, knew that if I didn't kick him off, climb out of the pool and into the empty chaise next to David that I was agreeing to something I didn't want to name. But I couldn't, because he wouldn't let go, and I didn't want him to. His hand tightened around my ankle, and I flattened my body against the slick tile wall. His other hand slipped between my legs, fingers brushed up against the elastic of my bathing suit bottom that cut into my hips, then under it. I was glad my body was under ten feet of water.

Then just as suddenly, he surfaced beside me, wiped his eyes, took my hand and held it against his stomach, then slid it further down. "Helena," he said, "It's not my choice anymore. My body doesn't lie." He gathered a fistful of my tangled hair and tugged me closer to him. I shivered in fear, wonderful fear, because he wanted me, wasn't fighting it, and I felt that wash over me, into me, easily, like light through air. I took a deep breath and dove underwater, down and down and down to the bottom of the pool to clear my head. When I came up for air, he was gone.

It was a mind-body problem.

That night in bed, David curled around me from behind and pushed his hips against me, the sign he wanted to make love. I slipped out of my panties, tucked them under the pillow, pulled him on top of me and then slipped away from him, detached mind from body, felt nothing, and thought:

you are married, you have a grown daughter, you already have a life, David is a good man, he loves you, you love him. It was the truth. I kissed him hard and sighed.

But then I thought: you can detach body from mind with Ethan, and once you have worked through desire, can come back to your mind, back to David. This, too, was the truth. Two separate hemispheres: one half acts, while the other remains perfectly unconscious. My body no longer seemed fixed, but was changing. I was afraid of what it might become.

One afternoon, Dede traipsed in with Rebecca to her lesson and sat on the couch, perched on the edge like a crow, and cawed at her daughter. "Bravo. Good one. Wrong note there. Beautiful. Too fast. Too slow. Ouch."

Rebecca turned to her mother after every comment and glared. "Mom, shut up. You're making me mess up." Rebecca was clumsy, her fingers knotted, shuffling, skipping notes, banging heavy on the keys. She was seething and there was nothing I could do since this was not about Rebecca and her mother, but about Dede and me. I had to wait out the hour, not interfere.

After the lesson, Dede held Rebecca in front of her, hands on shoulders, twirling her ponytail around and around a hand, claiming ownership, marking her territory in mine.

"So, Helena, how is she progressing?"

"I think you made her nervous today, Dede. She's usually much more focused. Right kiddo?" I smiled at Rebecca but she didn't smile back. She knew that I had ceded something to her mother, hadn't protected her hour of freedom.

"What about Ethan?" Dede asked, enunciating each word with care. "He won't play for me at home." For a moment, her face went flat and soft, but then gathered tight again.

Rebecca looked up at her mother, yanked her hair away. "He plays for me when you're not around. He's afraid you'll laugh." She giggled. "You know what I catch him doing?"

I shook my head, afraid that somehow he might have revealed me in a gesture, in a note.

"He sits at the piano, eyes closed, and runs his fingers up and down the keys without making any sound. And he sways and rocks back and forth, like he can hear it but can't play it yet." Rebecca beamed at her secret discovery, proud that she witnessed her father's rapture, but I wanted to say *No, go back, don't say it because it will be taken from him, ground into dust.*

But it was too late. Dede shook her head, then tittered, "He's no Beethoven. He's a husband and father with a daughter to put through college." She was saying this *to* Rebecca but *for* me.

When I could no longer hear their diesel Mercedes chugging down the street, I sank into the couch and closed my eyes. I knew she would use this against him, would laugh at him later that night as they were arranging themselves in bed, shifting to their proper sides after the quick tumble of sex that would provide the proof of their marriage, of love and fidelity. "I hear you're becoming a regular genius," she might purr, rolling the "r" around her mouth like a stone. She'd sit on top of him, legs clamped around his, holding him still. She would need to make him hers again, need to reel him back home, and would say, "So Liberace, maybe you need a sequined suit for the fall recital?" She would laugh, to show him she was joking, but he would fold up inside, turn on himself, see himself as she saw him: middle-aged, foolish, pathetic. I wanted to claw her eyes out in advance, ward off the attack I knew would happen.

Instead, I pulled out Rebecca's Rolodex card, found his office number Dede had listed as an emergency contact, and called. I told him to meet me at the Gold Coast Motor Lodge in Great Neck at eight. David supervised interns at the hospital until midnight. I left it to Ethan to come up with a story for Dede.

This is how I made sense of what I was about to do on the too-short drive in the empty lane, traffic bumper-to-bumper in the other direction, every stoplight a green: if only for one small smidgen of time, nothing really against the rolling years of the rest of our lives, I wanted to preserve our affair before it was renamed adultery by Dede or David or the smug tongue-waggers sprawled out on chaises at the club. Before Ethan realized how truly awful his fingers sounded bumbling up and down the keys, and that despite the silk blouses, the ginger body scrub, and the magenta toenails, I was not an exotic version of myself but the same staid, middle-aged Helena of the mixed-doubles set. Before I realized that my body, bared, was bound to disappoint as was this amateur staging of passion between two people who didn't really desire each other, but merely desired the return of desire.

The room was ordinary. No candles, wine, or flickering fire, just white walls, pastel landscape paintings, maroon bedspread. But then I kicked myself. This is not about romance, Helena. This is an affair. No ever after.

Ethan knelt in front of me, wrapped his hands around my waist and said, "I've never done this before."

He was afraid, nervous like me. But we had gone too far to not go through with it, had given ourselves over to it without question, without even really talking about it. I ran my hands through his hair, tugged him to me, made a conscious decision and offered him my desire, my body. Did he push me across the bed, unbutton my dress, unhook my bra, and ease my panties off with his teeth. Did I respond in kind?

We undressed quickly, alone, revealing all at once the fixed progression of our marriages: Ethan sat on the edge of the bed, dropping shirt, tie, blue boxers in a pile on the floor, switching off the bedside lamps; I burrowed under the scratchy polyester cover, sliding bra and panties under my pillow, hands crossed over my soft, flabby belly. We were no longer inside a scene of seduction, but inside each other's bedrooms, our respective failings laid bare.

When Ethan crawled under the covers, though, we made love like I had imagined—fast, furious, stunned love. But as he pushed into me and I rolled over him, I felt myself separate: part of me was there, beneath him, breath ragged, moaning with pleasure; the other part might as well have been hovering in the doorway, pushing a cart full of dirty towels, slivers of soap, and empty shampoo vials, embarrassed at having to witness this sad reenactment, this forced echo of desire. Afterwards, we moved away from each other and sat on opposite sides of the bed to dress. But Ethan turned to me, suddenly, and held my hand tight in his. "There isn't anything I wouldn't do for you," he said.

"You don't have to do anything."

"I want to wake up next to you every day, make love to you in a bed, our bed, on the beach, on top of your piano."

I laughed, tried to sound light, breezy, professional. "That could be difficult with David and Dede wandering around."

He sighed, "Maybe they'll fall in love. That way we can all be happy. I want to make you happy."

"I'm already happy," I said. My stomach turned over a hard lump of anger at the thought of David with Dede.

"Don't lie. I know you." His eyes pleaded with me, needing me to need him.

"What do you know? You know what I look like with my clothes off. You know I can play the piano and have a lousy drop shot. Now you know what I sound like when I come. You know my body, not me. You don't know me."

He smiled and kissed each of my fingers. "I want you. I know that. Listen. Rebecca will be okay with this. Dede," he paused, looked away, at the wall, at one of the ugly pictures, uncertain about whether he should actually be bringing up his wife's name in this moment. "She already suspects something. Nothing concrete, nothing she can put a name to, but it won't be a shock."

He was telling the truth. He had already imagined a life together for us, already rebuilt a studio with a piano bench built for two. But I didn't love him, I had only desired him, not as lover but as an adulterer thrown into the lion's den along with murderers and thieves. And I didn't even want him anymore.

Turning my back to him, I rolled my stockings up my legs. They snagged on a fingernail, tore. I balled them up and chucked them across the room. I would have to leave him without hope for recovery, for a future together. No midnight phone calls, no presents of lingerie, no clandestine meetings.

So I said, "I don't know you, Ethan. I don't want to. Not this way. We've fucked each other, once, like two kids in heat. Now it's time to get over it like two adults." I didn't really feel nothing, but I didn't feel love, so I tried to sound hard and mean, on the attack.

Ethan rose, had finished dressing faster than me, even

his ugly Jerry Garcia tie was properly knotted, no sign of stains. He said, "Lesson's over, class dismissed. That's it?"

I nodded.

"Well then, class is canceled."

"No," I said. "It doesn't have to be. I'm a professional. We *are* grown-ups in the end. We can handle it."

"I thought there was some law about shrinks sleeping with their patients." He was angry, I could see that, but that would pass as easily as my desire for him had passed.

"Dammit, Ethan. I'm a married piano teacher, but I'm also a woman whose body has its own logic and needs. I confused them with love but they aren't always identical. The body can make love, but not feel it. The body can feel love, and not make it. That's where I was confused. I can't separate making love to you from loving David." And I said David's name with conviction, certain that he belonged in this room, in this bed, in this discussion with me. He did, not Ethan.

Ethan came around to my side of the bed, put his hand on my shoulder. "Look at me."

So I did, and I saw he wasn't angry, just confused and sad.

"I can't separate you into two halves and pretend I only know one of them. So, no. I can't handle this. I can't sit next to you alone, pretend to play scales, all the while wanting to love you. Not fuck you. But to make love to you and keep you."

I was silent. There was nothing I could say that he would want to hear now anyway.

He left, and I watched him walk out the door, then emerge down below, into the parking lot. He didn't look up, just disappeared into his car and drove out into the snarl of rush hour traffic. I would give him five minutes, then I would leave, but soon he and I would be caught in it, alone in our cars, inching towards home, maybe even idling for a few moments beside each other, recognizing each other, and quickly turning away.

And it would continue like that. We would bump into each other at the club, at his daughter's spring recital, at the drycleaner in town, and we would fall away from each other as strangers, as if our bodies had never come together in this cheap room, in a wonderfully sad and separate moment, making a kind of love together. But not love, not that.

Renter's Guide
to the Hamptons

1. Nobody Stays in the City for the Summer

Finn and I had been looking for a summer rental since the previous July. The Fourth of July to be exact. We were driving to Jones Beach, attempting to fulfill the prerequisite of holiday fun, but sat in bumper-to-bumper traffic instead. It was our own fault; we woke at six-thirty, ready to tug on swimsuits, but preferred to remain naked, rolling around in bed until ten. Making love seemed more important, more urgent, than beating out the two hundred thousand day-trippers crawling out on the Long Island Expressway. In the backseat of the Volvo was a cooler packed with cold wine, paninis from Dean & DeLuca, wedges of brie and havarti, and oranges. The air conditioner was off, windows were rolled down, and we had stripped to our bathing suits, sticking to the seats with sweat.

For the first hour we sang along to the radio, resorted to twenty questions, even wrote down a list of prospective baby names for unconceived children, bickering over a Finn Jr. I said asserting progenitive authority through a name was inconsiderate of a child's independent identity; Finn, however, believed that a great name should not go to waste. By the second hour we had devoured the sandwiches and the oranges, spitting the pits at the cars alongside ours. By the third hour, Finn stopped talking, just banged his fist against the steering wheel, and muttered, "What a perfectly fucking great way to spend a day off." I think we turned back somewhere near Roosevelt Field. We never even came close to the Wantagh Parkway.

When we got back to the apartment, Finn yanked the Yellow Pages from the closet and scribbled down numbers for real estate agents.

"Isabel," he said, "we're moving up in the world. We're going to get a place in the Hamptons like everybody else we know. I'm sick of this back and forth in one day crap."

I laughed at Finn's face bisected by a sunburn, and wondered if it had affected his reasoning. I looked in the mirror over the couch. Mine was red too, only the opposite side.

"You want to buy a house now?" I asked. "Everyone's gone for the weekend."

"Not now," he said and kissed my forehead. "You need to start thinking long term. For next summer. In Amagansett near Glenna and Brad's."

"Finn, we can't afford that." I wondered how much concealer I'd need to rub on my face to even out the burn.

"Nobody stays in the city for the summer. We'll manage."

2. Just Because Your Friends Can Afford It...

Finn was an account executive at Foster and Thompson, head of the Bubble Trouble Gum account. I was a sixth grade teacher at the Pierce School. While we were able to live comfortably in an apartment on the sixteenth floor in a gleaming high-rise on Sixty-Third and York, garaged the Volvo for a ridiculous monthly fee, and started a savings account for future children, our jobs did not offer the convenience of a multiple-digit, disposable income. About the only perk of Finn's job was a case of fluorescent green "Mango Fandango a Mouth-Poppin' Tango" gum; and mine, faux Gucci scarves at Christmas. The Hamptons were strictly a day trip: picnic lunch, beach blanket, change of clothes for the long ride home.

Glenna and Brad had each been independently wealthy before they married. Glenna was actually Finn's friend first; they'd gone to Dartmouth together, and even briefly shared an apartment in the city after graduation. Of course, Glenna owned the apartment and Finn lived rent free, so that was part of the attraction. They were like brother and sister, and claimed to be the only two people who could live together and not get the least bit excited about each other's nakedness. I don't know that I really believed that, but I knew I didn't have to worry. We all married the ones we loved.

And Finn and I were in love, and earlier on, in lust; we could barely make it through a dinner party without managing to slip in an unobtrusive quickie in the bathroom, which is difficult to do in one-bedroom apartments in New York. It's not as if the bathrooms were tucked away in some second floor guest bedroom. But our friends were indulgent, just smiled, graciously holding their bladders.

Glenna's father had bought her the Amagansett house
as a wedding present a few years back. It was a Richard
Meier geometric design with a free-standing white chimney
that looked like an exclamation point from the driveway,
huge expanses of glass that rose up from the ground to
the third floor like sheets of ice, and a relentlessly white
color scheme: white walls, floors, ceilings, furniture, and a
whitewashed, blacktop driveway. Every morning, Glenna
carried around a sponge and bucket, inspecting the floors
and walls for careless footprints and fingerprints. The only
colors that found their way into the house were the view of
the ocean, the immaculate green sod, and the pots of fuchsia
geraniums that lined the decks. Guests quickly learned to
leave their shoes at the door and to pick up stray strands of
hair from the bathroom floor.

Every August, Finn and I spent the weekend at their
annual clambake, drinking margaritas, stuffing ourselves on
Maine lobster and African tiger shrimp, and once, skinny
dipping at midnight in the ocean. Glenna and I raced into
the water, dropping our towels at the last minute, diving
noisily beneath the surf; Brad and Finn strutted naked from
the deck, like a pair of displaced Greeks, chatting casually
as they crossed the sand. Glenna and I kept our eyes
focused on our respective husbands, but inevitably she'd
whisper, "Isabel, don't get me wrong. But I don't know how
I managed to live with Finn and never fuck him."

I laughed, watching her watch Finn, and felt an odd
sense of pride.

Then she sighed, "Brad, well, he just about keeps me
satisfied, but investment bankers just don't seem to have
the staying power." I glanced quickly. I didn't really see
the difference in size, but then, that's not really a precise
indicator for stamina; other factors like partner-pacing,
heart-lung fitness, and self-control seem more important.

And as the men waded in, Glenna rose up from the surf and floated on her back, her full breasts bobbing in the moonlight, her legs scissoring powerfully through the water. For a moment, I thought of *Jaws*, and swam over to Finn, holding him protectively by the waist. Brad swam under Glenna, up through her legs, and stood, with Glenna sitting on his shoulders. "How about a chicken fight," she called. Finn eyed Glenna, towering over all of us, and then swam under me. I kicked him away, keeping the water line at my armpits. Brad flipped Glenna backwards off his shoulders; Glenna and Finn linked hands, and circled around me, clucking. I ignored them. I knew when I was beat.

3. ... That Doesn't Mean You Can, Too.

That was the kind of summer Finn wanted. I didn't think he'd really follow through, placing it in the category of Finn's Whims: timeshare in Vermont, skeet shooting, leaving advertising for something more fulfilling, house in the Hamptons. But by the following week, women with names like Irena, Bianca, and Saira were leaving messages on our machine, gushing that they'd found the perfect rental house for us, and in one breath, quote prices, addresses, and famous neighbors. Finn played these messages over and over, nervously rubbing his fingers together, trying to conjure the money from the air.

"Twenty-five thousand, 64 Dune Hollow Road, Hollywood starlet next door. Oh, and I'll need a few character references for security."

He squeezed my shoulders and said, "Don't sweat it, Isa. We'll find a place yet. But it wouldn't hurt to look at this one."

I ran my hands down my stomach and thighs. I didn't really need to bump into anyone famous and perfect.

"And," Finn continued, "You never know what my Christmas bonus will bring."

I didn't have the heart to tell him that his bonus wouldn't make up the difference; it could buy a week's rental, maybe, if Mango Fandango started to sell; but I played along, not wanting to shatter him with the news that we would never make *Town & Country's* society page. No photographer would ever snap a candid photo of us at the Hampton Classic Horse Show. "You really want to get into that scene?" I asked. I didn't; it would be like the city all over again, only worse. I'd have to chat it up with Finn's ad-friends while picking my bathing-suit bottom out from my ass.

"It could be fun for a few months," he said, "an escape from the usual."

Finn longed for an impressive summer home. Beach front, long panes of glass that wrapped around the curves of the house, tiered decks, granite lap pool, and a roof that met at awkward angles. He thumbed through the pages of *Architectural Digest,* pointing out the respective merits of each carefully designed executive retreat and said, "Like this one, Isabel. With lots of light and a wet bar. That's what we need." He envisioned running for the Jitney, tie askew, martini in hand, the envy of his coworkers. I sympathized but our needs were not in agreement.

I imagined a small cottage with a sturdy L.L. Bean hammock strung between two towering pines. Purple morning glories creeping up lattice frames propped against the shingled eaves of the house. Something small, a bit dilapidated even. A place where a poet would live. Not that I wrote poetry, but I liked the idea of a place that could inspire beautiful words; I think I hoped it would inspire Finn to tuck flowery verses professing his love beneath my pillow. Our apartment and its uniform construction only inspired Finn to tack Post-It notes to the telephone: *Pick up dry cleaning! Buy new water filter! Call super about the noise in apartment above!* I didn't want cocktail parties and Little Neck clams, caviar in tomato cups, and foie-gras sandwiches. I didn't want to have to worry about running into supermodels on the beach. I didn't want to have to compare penis sizes of husbands.

Every other Saturday, for six weeks straight, we packed a thermos of black coffee, a bag of bagels, a detailed map of the East End of the Island, and left in the cold, dark, pre-dawn hours, driving two hundred miles round-trip, to look at rentals we couldn't afford, hoping that Irena, Bianca, or Saira had inadvertently tacked on a few extra zeroes to the list price.

4. Shop Around

We turned down countless offerings in East Hampton, Southampton, Sagaponack, Bridgehampton, Amagansett, Quogue, and Wainscott. It seemed that the only things we could afford in those areas were parking tickets. Saira and Irena eventually gave up; Bianca was determined to eke out a commission and persisted all the way through Christmas, when she left her last message: "My mother knows someone trying to rent a bungalow on the North Fork. Actually, they're trying to get rid of it. It sounds like a rustic gem that fits well within your price range. Outside of that, I have nothing left."

Finn hated it. No air conditioning, only ceiling fans that threatened to break loose and boomerang through the air. No pool to lounge in on a float with a cell phone and Bombay Sapphire martini. No curved windows or wet bar. The beach was a five minute drive. Instead, the bungalow sat on an inlet of the Long Island Sound, Dryden's Cove, unswimmable due to water mites. Swans waddled all over the property, honking and snapping, leaving behind trails of white poop. Finn said for five thousand bucks we might just as well pitch a tent on the East River.

I loved it. It wasn't luxury, but then it wasn't meant to be. Bianca said a fireman from Queens built it by hand about twenty years ago as his retirement home. He'd salvaged wood from burnt-out shells across the city, sanded the beams, and poured the foundation. Only one problem: he died in a fire, falling through weak boards on the top floor of some vacant building in the Bronx. His wife didn't want it, in fact, hated the country and was planning to move out West where her son lived.

The oak beams that crisscrossed the ceiling still bore wispy tracings of smoke scars. A dock stretched into the cove, sanded smooth of splinters. Alongside the house, blackberries grew in tangled bushes and the shingled eaves were naturally weathered, an effect caused by wind, salt, and time, not a sandblasting machine. In the hall closet, scratchy wool blankets were stacked neatly on the floor, wrapped in individual plastic bags with a mothball tucked between the folds. On the back shelf stood a row of fire extinguishers, ready at attention. I believed it would have been a happy home for the fireman, maybe even the wife, labored over, loved. I believed Finn and I could be happy there.

5. Location, Location, Location.

I told Glenna about the rental in the middle of our weekly manicure. She swiveled around in her stool, tugging her hand from the manicurist, and shook it at me. The manicurist scolded her. "Sit still, Miss."

Glenna gave her hand back, and with a withering look ordered, "Don't file them too short." She turned to me and continued, "Isabel, are you nuts? You'll be out of your mind by the end of the first week. Do you realize you're committing yourself to two and a half months of ticks, dirty clam shacks, and virtual chastity?"

I swished my hand in the basin, letting the warm water submerge my wrist; my fingers had puckered and the cuticles looked gnawed. I didn't feel like discussing it anymore. "It'll be restful," I said. "No cable, no takeout, no perfectly sculpted bodies." I glanced in the mirror sucking in my stomach, regretting the past few months of ramen noodles, Chinese, and pizza. Finn had been working late on a brand review for the gum company; I ate dinner alone, curled up in front of the television, grading spelling tests to the latest movie-of-the-week. The silk teddies had been retired to the back of the closet in favor of boxer shorts and tee-shirts. Needless to say, I didn't feel up to competing with the likes of Glenna, whose personal trainer, Juan Carlos, coached her through thousands of sit-ups each week. I did not have a naturally high metabolism, or the money to get my boobs sculpted, thighs sucked, butt and tummy tucked, cheeks hollowed, or lips plumped. Besides, I'd seen the After pictures of women whose silicone implants had floated to their shoulders; instead of Playboy perfection they wound up looking like hunchbacks. And liposuction could even kill you. So what if your thighs under your silk dress under the coffin lid were smooth and slim?

Glenna blew on her nails, now a gleaming red, and held them up to the light, inspecting for dust and smudges. "Look, Isa, why don't you spend July at our place. Brad'll be gone on a business trip. He'd be happy I had company."

The manicurist asked me to pick a color. I chose Barely

Pink. "It's just that Finn and I need some time alone. There's too many distractions in the Hamptons."

Glenna shrugged and slipped her hands under the heat lamp. "Ahh. I see. You mean too many female distractions. Can you trust him by his lonesome in the big city during the week?"

"You trust Brad don't you?"

She laughed and told the manicurist she needed another layer of topcoat.

One night in May, after Finn and I made love and were going about the business of arranging blankets and pulling on socks and underwear, Finn switched off the light, and sat on the edge of the bed, his back turned.

"I'm not finished getting dressed," I said, reaching for the switch.

"Don't," he said, "I can't talk with the light."

"What do you mean?" Light-sensitivity had never been a factor in our conversations before. I groped for the boxers and tee-shirt that had fallen to the floor.

Finn cleared his throat. "Don't you think sex has gotten a bit predictable lately?"

"We always seem to have fun. Even if we're not skyrocketing off the charts every time, it's always good."

He shrugged.

"Finn, if something's wrong with our sex life, if you're not satisfied, you need to tell me. But I thought that we were okay, better than okay even."

"That's not what I'm getting at," he said, and opened the night-stand drawer, pulling out something that flashed silver. Then he dropped a pair of handcuffs in the middle of the mattress.

We looked at them for a few minutes. Finn didn't say

anything, just acted as if he had no idea how they came to fall from his hands.

Finally I picked them up; the inside bands were lined with padded black velvet, several spots were rubbed out to a smooth sheen. "Where did you get them?" I asked, snapping open the left cuff and placing it around my wrist.

Finn stared at my hand; I snapped the cuff closed and he looked up. I think he was confused that I was taking it so well. "At this place near work. Exotic Cabaret. You don't have to worry, though, it's upscale."

"Finn, I'm not really worrying about the clientele at the moment," I said, which was a lie, because all I could think of was Finn in leg irons and leather underpants, led around by some dominatrix named Octopussy, to a seedy backroom for a test run.

He took my hand and ran his fingers over the cuff. "We don't have to. Only if you feel okay about it. They don't lock, so you can always get out."

I pushed aside his fingers and held my arm up in the light. The cuff slipped down to my elbow and I shivered; the metal was cold despite the velvet accessory. I didn't know what I felt. On the one hand, he was telling me that sex hadn't been okay for him, and I wondered how long he'd been bored. On the other hand, bondage was a side I'd never seen in Finn. I wondered how he found Exotic Cabaret, and if I should worry since Finn's idea of exotic sex was a quickie after reading the Sunday Travel Section; somehow he got excited over thatched huts in Thailand and safaris in Kenya. It made our apartment sex seem adventuresome. I offered to dress up like a harem girl, geisha girl, call girl. Kidding, of course. I didn't have the savoir faire to pull it off. But Finn said realism would ruin it.

I unsnapped the cuff, dropped it back on the mattress. "They won't solve anything. I'm willing to try, but you know they won't solve anything."

He looked hurt, then angry, and shoved the handcuffs back into the drawer. "Forget it. It was just an idea." He rolled over.

When I ran my hand down his back he flinched. "Finn, maybe a change of scenery will help. Out at the summer house we can have some time alone."

Finn snorted. "Isabel, why should some dump in the middle of nowhere change anything? I'd just as soon stay in the city to sweat out the summer. I mean, really. Who the hell has heard of Dryden's Cove anyway?"

"It's not a dump," I whispered, rolling towards the wall.

The handcuffs remained in the drawer.

6. *Only Bring What You Need.*

On Memorial Weekend, we boxed up enough summer clothes to last me a few weeks, and Finn a few weekends. I checked out twenty books from the library, packed laundry baskets full of sheets, towels, pillows, tennis shoes, sandals, an alarm clock, a blow-dryer, and cleaning supplies; paper bags with canned food scavenged from the cabinets, half hunks of cheese, fruit, salami, bread, soda, and wine from the refrigerator, and the small kitchen television in bubble wrap.

"Jesus, Isa," Finn complained, on his third trip down to the car, "it's not like I can't bring anything you need with me next weekend."

I handed him a box filled with pots, pans, silverware, took the picture of the two of us at last summer's clambake from the refrigerator, peeled off the scotch tape, and slipped it in his back pocket. "You wouldn't remember this, not if you were in a rush. Besides, you're not going to want to carry stuff on the train. And what if I need something on Tuesday? You won't be out until Friday."

On the drive out, we stopped at the Kmart in Riverhead, buying six lounge chairs, an extra cooler, jumbo size shampoo, several tubes of sunscreen on sale, a float, and a bird feeder. I argued that it would be nice to have birds around the house. I made Finn pull over at an Army-Navy we passed and purchased a hammock, a kerosene lantern, an orange rain poncho, and a pair of binoculars. "To watch the birds," I explained. Finn said I was getting out of hand.

Bianca had warned that there wouldn't be much in the way of on-site comforts outside of the army-issue blankets and that we should be prepared to do a bit of cleaning in order to make the place habitable. She was right.

We tackled the bedroom, porch, and living room first, mopping and dusting, beating out the mattress, shaking the couch cushions, brushing out cobwebs and spider eggs. We cleaned the kitchen last. When we finished, we were dirty and smelly.

Finn took off his tee-shirt and wiped sweat from his forehead. I surveyed the corners of the refrigerator, wiping out the last of the green scum and pulled my shirt over my head. "You know Finn, it's not that bad once it's clean."

He stepped out of his shorts and smiled. "It is a bargain," he said, crawling over on his hands and knees. He kissed my belly, then pulled down my shorts and underwear. I slid down the now gleaming refrigerator door, wincing when my shoulder hit the handle.

Finn trailed his fingers up my thighs. "There's something to be said for a little elbow grease."

We made love on the unfamiliar linoleum, furiously spurred on by a spontaneity reminiscent of our bathroom adventures, smacking hard into a poorly placed table, our

rear-ends and backs sticking to the soapy residue of Mr.
Clean. We smelled of pine and lemons, not sex and sweat,
and were content. The wickedly tidy tumble of domestic
sex was a gratifying omen.

On Monday, I drove Finn to the Long Island Railroad
station in Patchogue. As he was getting out of the car I said
casually, "You know, you could bring those handcuffs with
you on Friday."

He looked down the tracks, at the train approaching
the station, and shrugged. "If I can find them."

"They're right where you left them."

"I'll look."

With a wave, Finn was gone. He forgot the handcuffs
the following weekend. I knew he would.

7. Remember: The Object Is to Relax

I quickly developed a weekday routine. I woke just after
dawn, strapped on ankle weights, and walked the six miles
round-trip to the beach. Usually I would collect bunches of
black-eyed Susans and Queen Anne's lace, pick out the ants,
arrange them in a vase on the porch. I was happy with the
thought that it didn't take much to make me happy. Finn
always said I was a challenge, said he wanted to be the one to
crack the code to my happiness. I told him happiness wasn't
analogous to some DNA code or anagram, and promised
I was easy. Lately, though, he said I was impossible, that
the only time I seemed happy was when I was alone at the
bungalow, and maybe I needed to start seeing my shrink
again. So I called Sheila, charged the hour-long phone-
therapy session to Finn's Visa, hoping in part, that he would
be happy upon receiving the bill, to see that I was working
out the problem. Sheila said my lonely happiness, though,

was a positive step. "Don't you remember how lonely and unhappy you were when Finn was working late? I don't think you should worry. Finn should."

I collected jars of mussel and cockle shells, which I set on tabletops; hollow horseshoe crab carcasses, which I hung on the porch wall, their sharp pointed sturdiness masking their sun-baked brittle bodies; the bits of beach glass tumbled smooth against the rocks I kept in my pockets. I dutifully picked up plastic six-pack rings from the swash line, breaking them apart, sure that I was saving far-off dolphins from extinction.

The beach was quiet in the early mornings. Only the lifeguard, a red-haired girl about sixteen with a face tanned between her freckles, huddled on the stand, a sweatshirt stretched over her knees. We waved to each other but never spoke. One morning a boy, about her age, sat with her in the stand. They were arguing. Her hands were bunched in the pockets of the sweatshirt, fists ready; her feet swung out and back, heels battering the wooden supports. The boy suddenly smacked his hand against the seat, jumped off, landing hard in the sand, and stalked away. The girl watched him limp out to the parking lot and then turned back, staring out at the Sound. I thought she was going to run after him, stop him, call him back when she climbed down from the stand, but she crashed into the water, flinging the sweatshirt behind, and swam out, arms and legs furiously chopping through the waves. I watched her from the shore in envy.

I started a garden along the stone wall that ran around the property. I weeded and raked and bought seeds and gardening tools at the feed store, along with a knee cushion to kneel on in the dirt. Finn said I was wasting my time, that it wasn't as if improving the place would knock off anything from the rent. But that wasn't the point. It was the first time I'd started anything from seed that actually grew. I'd tried to grow a window herb garden back in the city, Magic Sprout Instant Herbs, pouring a half a cup of water into the pot each morning. I waited, imagining fresh basil, chives, and oregano winding their way up the window pane, to no avail. Magic Herbs like Sea Monkeys were designed to make the gullible feel incompetent of even the simplest of life-giving tasks.

But my summer garden took off; within two weeks, green stalks poked up through the dirt. By the fourth week, the chives were as long as wild grass and I was cooking with homegrown oregano.

This too: I hung a rainbow windsock off the dock and my laundry on a clothesline that connected the house to a neighboring pine. I didn't care if anyone saw my underwear waving in the breeze.

On weekends, Finn was restless. We went on walks, played tennis, sprawled across damp towels at the beach, made love on top of sandy sheets, and all he could say was, "There's nothing to do out here but sit around." On Sunday mornings he was predictably angry: Mr. McIntyre, our neighbor, gunned his lawn mower at the first signs of light. He had two acres to mow before ten, when he and Lottie, his wife, had to be at church. Mr. McIntyre was in the choir and practiced his hymns while he mowed; whenever he cut the motor, after running over a branch or rock, a verse of "My Lord Is My Rock And Savior Almighty," drifted up through the open windows. I didn't mind the noise, in fact, I welcomed it; alarm clocks seemed crude in comparison to McIntyre's moral weight.

Finn grunted, "Doesn't he know it's fucking Sunday, the day of rest?" and buried his head beneath the pillow. Finn liked to sleep in on weekends, liked his *Times* in bed with a mug of coffee on the night stand and my body wrapped in silk, pressed against the length of his. Since we didn't have home delivery of the *Times* and since I couldn't lounge in bed while listening to the Puritan serenade, Sunday morning sex had fallen by the wayside in favor of my walks to the beach. Besides, I found that I had gotten used to having the early hours to myself, out of bed, away from Finn.

It's not that I didn't want to make love, press my body into his, open myself up to him on weekends. But it was. I thought often about the red-haired lifeguard and her solitary swim.

Finn took the train out Friday evenings after work and left Sunday afternoon. For the rest of the week, I woke to an empty house, a mattress that seemed endless, a day that was mine. It was a strange feeling to be thirty, happily married for three years, contemplating children, and wondering if Lucy and Desi had it right with their twin beds. I called Sheila one Sunday evening, after Finn had left and said all I felt was strangely relieved; she said it was about time I realized marital bliss wasn't all it was cracked up to be, and that if apartments weren't so ridiculously expensive, she'd recommend two bedrooms and separate baths to all her female clients.

8. Entertaining Should Be a Casual Affair

Glenna drove up from Amagansett one afternoon for lunch, carrying a bottle of chardonnay and a basket of strawberries. "For you," she said, raising her sunglasses and pecking my cheek. "A housewarming gift." I gave her the grand tour, and she nodded enthusiastically until we reached the bathroom. She took one look at the unscrubbable mildew that filled the cracks between the brown and yellow tiles and chided, "I hope you changed the toilet seat. You never know whose ass has sat on it."

I set up a pair of aluminum folding chairs on the dock, brought out a tray of tuna sandwiches.

"Where did you get the tuna?" Glenna asked.

I thought it was an odd question; tuna fish usually meant canned Bumble Bee found on the shelves of most supermarkets. I didn't think that was the answer she would want to hear. "I forgot the name of the place."

"There's a wonderful fish market in Amagansett. The fish are always fresh. No chance of week old tuna that's for sure," she continued, opening the bottle of wine. "But I suppose you have a good local market, too." And then we toasted. "To al fresco dining," she said.

I found myself listening to a half-hour monologue of Hamptons' gossip. I didn't really know any of the people she was talking about, outside of some of the bona fide celebrities she'd spotted topless on the beach, sloppily dressed in dirty sweatpants in town, in flagrante delicto at a cocktail party. She sipped her wine, nibbled at the ends of her sandwich, never really taking a full bite, and continued, "Our new neighbors. Wait'll you hear this one. I was walking down the beach one night, and hear this shrieking so I sneak around the side for a better view. Get this, Isa. The guy is tied up naked to the diving board, and the girl is standing over him wearing a mask, cracking a whip, and he has a very obvious erection, sticking straight up, about the only thing I could see clearly. She cracks the whip against the diving board and he shrieks. Again and again, without his skin ever licked by the damn thing."

I laughed at the story, light-headed from the wine and sun, and sat on the edge of the dock, skimming my feet along the water. "What do you think about that kind of thing?" I asked. There seemed to be a more interesting, less preposterous, propless ways to spend an erotic evening at home.

Glenna poured more wine. "The psychodrama I can dispense with. But a good tight blindfold and pair of cuffs...."

I peeled the crust from my sandwich and threw it at a swan paddling lazily a few yards out. It swam over, circled the crust, then thrust its head beneath the water, snapping the bread up in its beak.

"Of course," she said, "Brad's not really into that kind of thing. He can be such a prude. His idea of down and dirty is on all fours. Woof woof, yawn yawn. But Finn, now he's the kind of guy with imagination. He looks like he might like to give a good spanking."

"He never looked that way to me," I said.

"Trust me," Glenna said, "he was a wild man in college. The stories I heard...." She threw her sandwich into the water. Bits of tuna floated across the surface, the bread began to sink. The swan paddled over to pick through the remains.

Glenna had a habit of embellishing the truth when she was drunk, but still, I didn't like the idea of her and Finn sharing sexual secrets. As I studied her, twirling her expertly highlighted hair, swigging the wine, I realized I didn't have to like Glenna. Not at all.

Glenna stood up, announcing suddenly that she had to get back for a late afternoon round of golf. She kissed me goodbye, drained her wine glass, and laughed, "Don't worry, Isabel. I know just the place that can help you out. Sort of an S & M shop, but very civilized. You'll see. In the mean time, keep an eye out for a care package."

The brown-paper wrapped box arrived the following week. Inside, an assortment of toys—French tickler, blindfold, and handcuffs—similar to Finn's, but the velvet looked new. A card was at the bottom, buried beneath the layers of tissue paper: *Just a little starter kit for a new initiate. Cheers! Glenna.* The Customer Service number? 1-800-Cabaret. So very discreet and upscale in the fine print.

Glenna and Brad swore by Bloody Marys. "Just the thing to put a spin on your morning," Brad said. We were "brunching" at their place one Saturday afternoon under the white pagoda by the pool, passing plates of scrambled eggs, lox, crab and dill quiche, caviar, fresh bagels, a hollowed watermelon filled with fruit salad, and several pitchers of Bloody Marys. After we finished eating, Glenna tipped her chair back into the sun, rolled down the straps of her bathing suit, and ate an occasional chunk of melon. Brad, now drunk, walked down to the beach, carrying a pitcher and a glass, to watch the late surfers. Finn took seconds of everything and murmured through his muffin, "Now this is the way to live. Everything you'd ever need to be happy." I watered Glenna's geraniums which were wilting in their pots of dry soil.

"Isa, you don't need to do that. I have a gardener you know," she said.

"But they're dying. It'll just take a few minutes."

Glenna nudged Finn. "When did Isa develop such a green thumb?"

Finn laughed. "It keeps her occupied when I'm not around during the week."

I turned on the hose and filled the watering can. It took fifteen refills to wet down all thirty pots. But I listened when Glenna asked Finn if he thought she should get a breast enlargement. She explained that Brad didn't care one way or the other and she needed a man's opinion before going through with it. She unwrapped her sarong, which fluttered to her feet, rolled her bathing suit to her waist, and spun around, pausing for a profile and head-on view. "See," she said, cupping her hands beneath breasts, "I'm beginning to sag. They could be a bit rounder, don't you think?"

Finn looked her over, slowly, and shook his head. "They're perfect."

I pretended to ignore them as I broke off the dead flowers, scattering the brown leaves and petals across the deck which was painted a high gloss slippery white. Not a very considerate architectural choice. One misstep with a wet foot, and a person could split their head open.

But I couldn't help looking at her breasts, which upon consideration, weren't so perfect.

9. Be Prepared For Rainy Days and Bouts of Cabin Fever

Fourth of July weekend, a cold front drifted down from Canada, bringing torrential rain, fifty-degree weather, and thirty-mile wind gusts. The fireman had failed to winterize the bungalow, so on Saturday, Finn and I sat in bed, wrapped in the scratchy blankets, and watched reruns of *Three's Company*. We tried to play Monopoly which had been left behind by a previous renter, but half of the cards were missing and we both ended up bankrupt within an hour. We had sex on the theory that body heat would help us warm up, but shivered all the way through. It was miserable.

I had convinced Finn that despite the dire weather reports, it would be romantic to hole up in the bungalow for the weekend. We could picnic in bed. Over the phone, he sounded skeptical, but I thought it was due to the phone battery running out. I was late picking him up at the train;

visibility was about ten feet in the storm. He was angry and cold; his new summer sport coat from Burberry's was damp and wrinkled. I told him he was stupid to wear a five hundred dollar blazer when he knew beforehand it was going to pour.

He folded the blazer in half and stretched it across the backseat. "I should have stayed in the city. A weekend apart wouldn't kill us," he said.

I stared intently ahead, hands gripping the steering wheel, unsure of the curves of the road that on a clear day I had memorized. The weather was screwing up my reflexes. "Finn, we already spend the week apart," I reminded, slowing almost to a stop as we came over a rise in the road.

He turned the radio from the news station I'd had on, in hopes of hearing a weather update, to a rock station. "The separation is your decision, Isa. Not mine. You could've come into the city for the weekend."

I turned off the radio. "When did we start calling this a separation?"

He laughed. "Don't be so serious. But we may as well call a spade a spade. We are separated from Sunday to Friday." He turned the radio back on and dropped his hand across my neck. I think in reassurance.

I chewed on my lip and said, "You don't have to be so technical about it."

On Sunday, Glenna called. "Now don't tell me you two are having fun in the rain. Why don't you drive out here? At least we can all keep each other company. I'm so lonely without Brad." Brad was in Hong Kong for the week on business. Glenna liked to play the part of lonely housewife. I knew she didn't really mind since Brad always brought her back suitcases full of Chanel knockoffs.

Finn barbecued steaks under the pagoda. I stripped corn husks. Glenna made a Caesar salad. We finished two bottles of wine before dinner. We ate in the living room; long white taper candles softly glowed from a candelabra; Puccini played on the stereo. Finn and I sat on the white couch, Glenna sat cross-legged on the floor. I warned Finn not to spill the red wine. Glenna said not to worry, the couch was Scotch-guarded.

Glenna wore a long white dress that flared at her ankles. Her skin was dusted with gold shimmer powder. She wasn't wearing a bra.

"If I didn't know any better," I said, "I'd think you were trying to seduce us."

Glenna laughed and tossed her hair over her shoulder. "I need to have a little fun when Brad's away. And since you're friends, that makes it even more interesting."

Finn cleared his throat and announced the storm was letting up.

"Good," Glenna whispered, leaning her breasts into the coffee table, "that means we can go swimming later. First let's get good and drunk."

Throughout dinner I noticed that things seemed a little odd, but couldn't tell if it was the wine that was skewing my perceptions or paranoia. What was odd was that Glenna and Finn seemed too comfortable without Brad. Without me, even. They told stories about Dartmouth, about the times they got drunk together, about the time they almost fooled around, but wound up passing out. I'd heard the story several times before, from both of them, and always laughed, especially when Glenna told the part about how she woke up in the middle of the night to Finn peeing in her closet, all over her shoes, mistaking it for the bathroom.

She said she didn't have the heart to wake him since he seemed so sure it was a toilet; he even tried flushing with the doorknob. But later that day, she dragged him to the mall and charged five hundred dollars worth of shoes on his credit card.

But this time, when Glenna said, "I guess that just shows you we were never meant to be lovers," and Finn looked at her, finishing the punch line, "Especially since it took me two years to pay off those damn shoes," they sounded lonely for each other, and I wondered if they really had passed out, or if that was an agreed upon lie meant, in good faith, to reassure Brad and me of the platonic nature of their friendship, but now only served to reinforce the weight and significance of the memory for them.

I realized that evening that I was quite willing to let Finn slip away from me for a few hours; for that one night I didn't mind being the bystander; it was a relief to not have to fight their solidarity. I think it was at the moment when Glenna tugged her dress over her head and raced down into the water, so certain that she would not be left to swim alone, that I decided not to follow. Finn looked at me, already stepping out of his madras plaid shorts, and asked, "You're not coming?"

"It's too cold." Which was the truth. Although the rain had stopped, the wind still whipped across the water.

Finn gave me a quick kiss and said he would be back soon.

I watched them through the long windows, my palm pressed against the cold glass. It was hard to distinguish who was who. All I could see was the whiteness of their skin against the dark water. And when they embraced? I didn't run out after them hurling insults, throwing punches. I finished my final glass of wine, brought the plates into the kitchen, wiped down the table, couch, muddy footprint

Finn left by the door, and handprint I'd left on the window pane. It was only after I was home, buried deep in the scratchy blankets, that I cried because I discovered I didn't care.

10. You're Paid Up Through Labor Day
So Be Sure to Make the Best of It

For the rest of the summer, Finn and I remained separated. Technically. We divorced a year later, not because of that night (in fact, we never even really talked about it, we just floated away from each other like pieces of driftwood) but because of the bungalow. I wanted to put in a bid to buy, Finn wanted to save for a place in the Hamptons, or a condo maybe in Montauk. And so we split, realizing we were ultimately incompatible. I kept the Volvo, he kept the apartment, which was fine by me, considering what I later found out from Brad: all summer, Glenna and Finn had been meeting there for weekday trysts. I put two and two together and realized Finn's handcuffs probably hadn't gone to waste. Finn and Glenna moved in together by the following July.

We split the savings and the college fund for our never-to-be-conceived children. Finn bought a Saab convertible. Not very practical for the city since the insurance alone must be killing him, not to mention parking. But I'm sure he's happy driving out to the Hamptons, top down, Glenna handcuffed to his side, and well-trained to live carefully in her immaculate white house.

I took my half of the money and put a down payment on the bungalow. I worked out a deal with the widow who was only too happy to have the place taken off her hands. In fifteen years, barring any accidents, 6 Dryden's Cove Lane will be mine. The final mortgage payment will be made. I have big plans for the garden this summer. Cucumbers, peppers, tomatoes, and squash. And I hope to find the red-haired lifeguard, wrapped in her sweatshirt, perched in her stand, alone on the beach. I'd like to know her name.

Once I saw Finn and Glenna at the Central Park dog run of all places. Appropriate. I was careful not to let them see me; I wanted to observe them from a distance, judge their success by their un-self-conscious coupledom. They had a bulldog that they called Attila, probably AKC registered. Attila kept peeing in other dogs' water bowls. It was disgusting and selfish; they just stood by, oblivious as Attila lifted his tiny leg and squirted little spurts of piss into the clean water. I wanted to run the two of them out, humiliate them, sic all the dogs on them, the spaniels, retrievers, terriers, shepherds, the lone Great Dane, even the pug could get a firm grip on a kneecap. But I felt sorry for Attila, the beast that it was, for what it must suffer for peeing on their spotless floors. Besides, I was there with a date and his mutt Missy, who looked a little like a German shepherd crossed with a yellow Lab. We were still in the formative stages of our relationship, and I didn't think I was ready to handle the awkward introduction of an ex-husband.

I met Patrick at the Pierce School a few weeks earlier; a child psychologist, he was consulting on the new lower school building, and we talked one long afternoon, over hot pretzels and Cokes on a bench in the schoolyard, about what kind of classroom design I thought kids could be happy in. I was hooked.

I scratched Missy under the chin and she pressed her wet nose into my knee and rested her head in my lap. And I realized, as Glenna and Finn left the dog run, cursing at each other and at Attila who dragged behind, biting at his leash and their ankles, that the anger had passed, as quickly as it had happened. Three months, the length of a lease for a summer rental.

K erry Neville Bakken teaches at Allegheny College and lives in Meadville, Pennsylvania, with her husband and two children. Her stories have appeared in *Glimmer Train*, *StoryQuarterly*, and *Cimarron Review*. After growing up on Long Island, she earned degrees from Colgate University and the writing program at the University of Houston. *Necessary Lies* is her first book.